The Mardi Gras Mystery

Nancy stopped cold in her tracks, her eyes riveted to a point down the street. Ned turned and saw her staring. But before he could speak, she plunged into the crowd. She was trying frantically to reach something—or someone.

Nancy ran madly, shoving people aside as she battled her way up the sidewalk. Finally she stopped and leaned against a streetlight. She was breathing heavily. Ned was the first to reach her.

"What in the world made you run off like that?" he exclaimed. "Nancy? Are you all right? You look as if you've seen a ghost."

"Maybe I have," she said, still gasping for breath. "I know it sounds crazy, but I just saw Danielle Seaton—a woman who drowned fifteen years ago!"

Nancy Drew
Mystery Stories

Available from MINSTREL Books

81

NANCY DREW®

THE MARDI GRAS MYSTERY

CAROLYN KEENE

A MINSTREL® BOOK

PUBLISHED BY POCKET BOOKS

New York   London   Toronto   Sydney   Tokyo   Singapore

A MINSTREL PAPERBACK *ORIGINAL*

A Minstrel Book published by
POCKET BOOKS, a division of Simon & Schuster Inc.,
1230 Avenue of the Americas, New York, NY 10020

ISBN: 0-671-64961-2

Produced by Mega-Books of New York, Inc.

First Minstrel Books printing January 1988

10 9 8 7 6 5 4 3

J 99990 20407753

Contents

1

Welcome to Mardi Gras

"Hurry up, you two. I can hardly see Ned in this crowd."

Nancy Drew was fighting her way through the excited people who were getting off the plane in New Orleans. At the same time, she was urging her two best friends, Bess Marvin and George Fayne, to keep up with her. Nancy was following Ned Nickerson toward the waiting room. Ned was supposed to meet his Emerson College friend Brian Seaton, who had invited them to New Orleans for Mardi Gras week.

Nancy and her friends had jumped at the chance to go to the celebration of Mardi Gras. They were looking forward to a glorious week of parades, parties, shopping, and fun in one of the most romantic cities in the country.

But at the moment, Nancy felt as if she were a juggler. She was trying to keep Ned's red sweater in sight in front of her, while making sure Bess and George were still behind her. At last, Ned came to a halt and began shaking the hand of

1

another boy. Nancy breathed a sigh of relief. He had found Brian.

Nancy, Bess, and George fought their way through the crowd, finally catching up to Ned and Brian.

"Here we are," Ned said to Brian. "I told you we'd make it."

Brian smiled. He was sandy haired, tall, and tan, but neither as tall nor as handsome as Ned. He grinned charmingly at the girls, though, and they smiled back.

Ned began the introductions. "Nancy, Bess, and George," he said, pointing to each of the girls. "Brian Seaton, my friend and co-football star."

Nancy looked at Ned and laughed. "You're *so* modest, Ned Nickerson," she teased. "That's what I like about you."

Brian grinned again. "Pay no attention to him," he said. "I never do."

Nancy and her friends edged through the crowded airport toward the baggage area.

"It's going to be a great week," Brian went on. "I've got all kinds of things planned for us."

"Terrific," Nancy said. "I could use a week of fun."

"Yeah, that last case you solved was pretty tough," George said.

"It was pretty scary, too," Bess added with a shudder.

George looked at Bess and rolled her eyes. The two girls were first cousins, but they were total opposites. Tall, slim, brown-haired, brown-eyed George was athletic and energetic. Pretty, blond, blue-eyed Bess was slightly plump and a little lazy. She liked to avoid danger whenever possible. But even though they were different types, the cousins were close friends, loyal to each other and to their best friend, Nancy Drew.

"Well, at least that case is over," Nancy said.

"And Mardi Gras is here," said Ned happily.

"That's right," Brian said. "So let's not waste any time. But first I've got to pick up my father. I hope you don't mind. His French sports car is in the shop again."

"We don't mind," said Nancy.

"Great," Brian said, "because I've got something to show you. My father is over at our cousin Warren Tyler's house, and you won't believe what's there."

Nancy and her friends pulled their suitcases off the conveyor belt and followed Brian to the parking lot. He pointed to a shiny blue late-model sedan off to the right.

"We're going in the sedan," he said, "but your luggage will have to ride in that."

Parked next to the sedan was a black limousine. A gray-haired chauffeur was standing beside it. He helped Brian load the luggage inside, then drove off. Nancy and Ned climbed into the front seat of the sedan, while Bess and George piled into the back. Then Brian headed out of the airport.

Ned had told Nancy that Brian came from a wealthy family, but somehow Nancy hadn't expected anything like this. French sports cars, chauffeurs, limos . . . Brian's dad, Bartholomew Seaton, was some kind of businessman, Nancy

3

knew, but Ned had said that Brian didn't talk about his father very often.

As they drove down the highway, Ned and Brian began telling college stories. The girls looked at each other and rolled their eyes. When Nancy couldn't stand it any longer, she asked about the Mardi Gras activities.

"This was going to be a surprise," Brian said, "but I'll tell you anyway. Tonight's the big masked ball at the Silver Sail Yacht Club, and we're all invited. I've even picked out costumes for you. Ned gave me some hints. I hope I didn't mess up."

"Just as long as I don't have to be any kind of animal," said Bess.

"You can trust me," Brian answered. "Honest."

"But can we trust Ned," Nancy joked.

"You really have to ask that?" Ned kidded back.

"I can remember a few pranks . . ."

"Okay, okay," Ned interrupted. He turned to Brian. "Nancy's got a mind like a steel trap. Never tell her *anything* you don't want her to remember."

"A detective has to remember things," Nancy said with a laugh. "Give me a break!"

Then Bess asked, "By the way, Brian, what is this thing you're going to show us?"

Brian smiled mysteriously. "Well, I don't know if any of you like art, but there's been a really amazing discovery and it had to do with my family."

"What kind of discovery?" Nancy asked, her curiosity growing.

"There was an artist named Lucien Beaulieu who used to live and work in New Orleans. He died ten years ago," Brian said, as he steered the car off the highway and onto a side road. "He's pretty famous in New Orleans. He did a lot of street scenes around the city, and local portraits, that sort of thing. Anyway, you'll never guess what's been found—a portrait he did of my mother!"

Nancy raised her eyebrows. She exchanged a glance with Ned. Nancy remembered Ned once saying that Brian's mother was dead, and that she had died in mysterious circumstances.

"Your mother?" Ned asked carefully.

"Yes," said Brian. Then he added, "It's too bad my father didn't find the painting. He'd give anything to have it. But it was discovered by Warren Tyler. He's a second cousin of my father's. That's where we're going now. I'll pick my father up there and you can see the painting."

As they drove on, Nancy started to wonder about Warren Tyler and Mr. Seaton. If they were cousins, why didn't Mr. Tyler just give the portrait to Brian's father? Surely he must know how much it would mean to the Seatons. She also wondered how Mr. Tyler had gotten the portrait in the first place.

Brian's voice interrupted her thoughts. "Here we are," he said.

Warren Tyler's house was large and appeared to date back to the early part of the century. It

5

was in good condition for an old house, though the paint was beginning to peel in several places. Brian parked the car, then led the others across the large front porch. He walked into the house without knocking.

As they entered, they heard loud, angry voices coming from the living room. But the voices stopped quickly when Brian called, "Hello, Dad!"

A tall man stepped into the foyer, looked at his watch, and said brusquely, "You're late!"

"The airport was a mob scene." Brian looked uncomfortable but went on stiffly, "Dad, I want you to meet Ned Nickerson, Nancy Drew, Bess Marvin, and George Fayne. My father, Bartholomew Seaton."

Mr. Seaton shook hands quickly with Ned, then nodded at the girls. He was a big man, taller than Brian, and slightly overweight. Dressed neatly in a three-piece suit, he looked well groomed, with every hair in place. Nancy was sure she had never seen a sterner man. She felt slightly sorry for Brian.

At that moment, another man followed Mr. Seaton into the foyer. Brian's father didn't bother to introduce him, and Nancy sensed a coolness between the two. She also noticed a slight scowl on the face of the second man.

Brian introduced him to Ned and the girls. As Nancy had guessed, the man was Warren Tyler. He appeared to be the same age as Mr. Seaton— about forty-five—but he was balding and not nearly as well dressed.

"We understand you have a very exciting discovery here," she said, giving Tyler a friendly smile.

Tyler raised his eyebrows. "Word travels fast," he replied. "Only I wouldn't say exciting is the best way to describe it."

"I'd say ironic is more like it," Brian's father said sarcastically.

Bess cleared her throat nervously. "Could we see the painting, Mr. Tyler?" she asked. "The story sounds so interesting."

Warren Tyler seemed to loosen up a bit. He smiled at Bess and nodded. "Of course. Brian, you know where the painting is. Why don't you show it to your friends?"

Brian led Nancy and her friends into a high-ceilinged living room. At the far end of the room, over a marble fireplace, hung a portrait in an ornate frame.

Brian flipped a switch and the painting was bathed in light from all sides. Nancy and her friends looked on in wonder.

"This," Brian said dramatically, "is *Danielle's Dream.*"

Nancy felt spellbound by the creation before her. And she knew the others felt the same way. The painting was absolutely beautiful. It showed a woman kneeling in a field of wildflowers with a red barn in the background. The woman might have been thirty years old, maybe a little older. She wore her long black hair loose, and it cascaded over her shoulders like a waterfall. The woman was smiling, but she looked fragile.

It was her face that was really extraordinary. The face was not only beautiful, but haunting. It

7

seemed to contain a hidden sadness, perhaps even pain. The artist had captured this feeling mostly in the dark eyes that stared into the distance. And he had somehow portrayed a feeling of hope and despair at the same time.

Along with the beauty of the haunting woman, *Danielle's Dream* also contained an element of mystery. Nancy could feel it calling out to her.

"This woman is your mother?" she asked Brian.

He nodded.

"She's beautiful," Nancy said. "Absolutely beautiful."

Brian sighed. "I wish I remembered her. But I don't really. She died fifteen years ago. I was only four. I remember little bits and pieces, I guess, but not what she looked like."

Nancy nodded in complete understanding. Her own mother had died fifteen years before, when Nancy was three years old. Since then, she had been raised with love and affection by her father and the Drews' housekeeper, Hannah Gruen. Still, Nancy sometimes wished she could remember more about her mother. She knew how Brian felt.

"My dad didn't keep any pictures of my mother," Brian continued. "He was so upset when she died that he locked away every single photo of her. He's never told me where they are. Some people think that's weird, but I can understand how he felt. I think he's sorry now about what he did, though. He'd really like to have this portrait. He's willing to buy it from Warren."

8

"Why won't Mr. Tyler sell it to him?" asked George.

"Or even give it to him?" Nancy added. "You said Mr. Tyler is your dad's cousin, right?"

"Second cousin," Brian replied. "But it's not, um, that simple." Brian shifted from one foot to the other. "Dad and Warren Tyler don't get along at all. You see, Warren was once in love with my mother. He and Dad both wanted to marry her. My father won, Warren lost." Brian shrugged. "Warren's still mad because he lost, and Dad is mad because he knows Warren never stopped loving my mother, not even after she got married."

"Wow," said Nancy softly.

"So," Brian went on, "there's no way Warren will give this painting to Dad. He wouldn't sell it if he was down to his last nickel and my father offered him a million dollars for it."

"A matter of principle," said George.

"No, a matter of sentiment," Brian replied. "This painting is all Warren has of my mother."

"But your father was *married* to her!" Bess exclaimed. "That's not fair."

"Where did Mr. Tyler find the portrait, anyway?" Ned asked Brian.

Brian smiled. "Listen to this. The story gets weirder. Warren heard about this farm that was for sale outside the city—"

"Outside New Orleans?" interrupted Bess.

"Yes. And he thought it might be good to own some property there. He'd heard that some big developer was going to build a shopping mall in that area. So he found a farm for sale and it turned out to be Lucien Beaulieu's."

"The artist," Nancy said.

"Right," Brian said with a nod. "Beaulieu had passed away several years before and the farm had just been standing empty. Warren bought the farm cheap, thinking he could sell it for a lot more money later. Anyway, one day not long ago he went out to take a look at the farm. He was prowling around the barn when he came across four paintings hidden away in a stall. Three of them were street scenes of New Orleans. The fourth was *Danielle's Dream.* He couldn't believe it, and neither could my dad."

"What a story," said Bess dreamily.

"Where are the other paintings?" asked George.

"Oh, Warren sold them to some art dealer. Mr. Koch," Brian replied. "Koch has a gallery here, and he couldn't wait to get his hands on these 'lost' Beaulieu originals. He paid a lot of money for them. Of course, he's dying to buy *Danielle's Dream*, but I guess he'll never be able to."

Brian was interrupted by his father.

"Come on, Brian," he said. "Are you and your friends ready? I'm late for an appointment."

Nancy and her friends thanked Warren Tyler for letting them see the painting. Then, they went outside to the car. Brian started to slide in behind the wheel, but his father held him back.

"I'll drive," he said gruffly.

The group squeezed into the sedan, the girls in the back, Brian between Ned and his father in the front. Mr. Seaton threw the car into gear and

10

spun away from Tyler's home. Nancy could tell that both Brian and his father were upset, and for a few minutes, no one spoke. Then Bess and George began to talk about the costume ball. But Nancy continued to watch Brian's father.

Mr. Seaton was gripping the steering wheel so hard his knuckles had turned a ghostly white. When he finally spoke, it was as if he were thinking the words and didn't really mean to say them.

"I've got to have that painting," he said. "And I'm going to get it . . . *somehow*."

2

Stolen Dream

Bartholomew Seaton's words created even more tension in the car. Bess and George stopped talking. No one spoke as they headed down a long, winding road toward Brian's home. A wooden road sign finally broke the ice. It read Entering Bat Hollow.

"Now, *that* sounds scary," Bess said, with a shiver. "Are those the kind of bats I think they are?"

Brian laughed. "They aren't the kind you play baseball with."

"Funny, I didn't see any signs for Transylvania," George teased.

Even Mr. Seaton laughed at that.

"Don't worry," Brian said. "You probably won't see a real live bat the whole time you're here. The name goes back years. There are a bunch of caves and tree hollows near our property, and bats live in them. But they only come out at night. You rarely see them during the day."

The car pulled into a huge circular driveway,

and Nancy got her first glimpse of the Seaton house. All thoughts of haunted castles and bat-infested belfries left her head when she saw the magnificent mansion sitting atop a slight rise. A nineteenth-century building, it either had been perfectly preserved or had been restored to its original beauty.

Around the front side of the house, huge round columns framed a long porch and a second-floor balcony. Nancy marveled at the hand-carved railing around the balcony and the sculptured window frames.

Bartholomew Seaton stopped the car and prac-tically jumped out. He ran inside. Brian started to follow him but noticed that his guests weren't coming. They were all standing by the car and staring at the mansion.

"Hey, what's up?" Brian asked, as he walked back toward the car. "It's a big place, but it doesn't bite."

Nancy laughed. "That's a funny thing to say about a place called Bat Hollow, but really, it's just that it's so beautiful."

"Well, let's go inside then," Brian said.

When they entered the house they were greeted by the same gray-haired man who had picked up their luggage at the airport. Brian called him Bosworth.

The interior of the mansion was every bit as grand as the outside.

The rooms were large and beautiful. The high-ly polished floors were covered with Oriental rugs. The door frames and the floor and ceiling

13

moldings were hand carved. And huge oil paintings hung everywhere. Mr. Seaton seemed to be a serious art collector.

"Okay, okay," Brian said. "We'll have time for sightseeing later. Let me show you your rooms so you can get settled. Then I'll tell you about the ball and show you your costumes."

Brian led the way to the second floor, where each of his guests was given a separate room. Nancy's, Bess's, and George's rooms had canopy beds and dressing tables with lighted mirrors. Ned's room overlooked the swimming pool in the rear.

"I think I could get used to this kind of life," Bess whispered to Nancy.

Nancy unpacked leisurely, pausing several times to look out the window at the lawn and flower gardens. When she was finished, she left her room and ran into Ned, who was coming out of his room.

"I told you this would be a perfect vacation," Ned said. "This is a great way to unwind. I can sure use a week of relaxation and fun. So can Bess and George. So can *you*."

Nancy and Ned walked slowly down the stairs toward the living room. "I'll tell you one thing though," Ned said quietly. "I feel bad for Brian. I wouldn't want Mr. Seaton for my father."

"Me neither," Nancy agreed. "But Mr. Seaton was in a bad mood when we got to Mr. Tyler's. That business with the portrait must be painful for him. I wonder what he's going to do."

"Oh, no. Come on, Nancy. Stop being a detective for a while. We're here to relax."

14

"You're right," Nancy said. "Let's forget about it."

"Good. I shouldn't have brought it up. It's just that I like Brian so much. Mr. Seaton made me a little angry."

"You're a good friend, Ned Nickerson," Nancy said.

When Nancy and Ned reached the living room, Bess, George, and Brian were already there. Brian had stacked several large boxes on a table. He was smiling broadly. Outwardly, his father's behavior didn't seem to bother him. Maybe he's good at hiding his feelings, Nancy thought.

"You're late," Bess said to Nancy and Ned. "You're keeping me from seeing my costume."

"That's a switch," Nancy teased. "It seems as if we're usually waiting for you!"

George laughed. "You'd better believe it. I've been waiting for Bess all my life."

"Okay, okay," Bess said, grinning good-naturedly. "Two against one isn't fair. But, right now, I can't wait to start having fun at Mardi Gras!"

"That's just how I feel," Brian said. "So on with the costumes. Bess first."

Brian lifted the cover off the top box and carefully removed a costume.

"I love it!" Bess cried.

The costume was a formal gown, the kind worn by Southern belles in the nineteenth century.

"Miss Scarlett O'Hara," Brian said, referring to the heroine of *Gone with the Wind*.

"Oh, Brian," Bess said, beaming. "You

15

couldn't have made a better choice! I can't wait to put it on."

While Bess continued to admire her costume, Brian opened the other boxes. He presented Ned and Nancy with elaborate costumes of the eighteenth century. Ned and Nancy were to be the French king Louis XVI and his queen Marie Antoinette.

"It's hard to believe people wore these things two hundred years ago," Ned remarked.

"Not people, royalty," Nancy reminded him.

"Whatever," Ned replied. "These are great."

"Now for George," Brian said. "Try this one on for size."

"What's that?" Bess asked.

"It's a Cleopatra costume," Brian replied, grinning.

"I love it," George said. "I always wanted to be an Egyptian queen."

"How about you, Brian?" Ned asked. "What are you going to wear?"

"I'm staying local," Brian answered. "I'm going as that infamous pirate of old New Orleans, the swashbuckling Jean Laffite!"

"Terrific," Ned said. "If things get dull, you can challenge someone to a sword fight."

"Believe me, things never get dull at a Mardi Gras ball," Brian replied.

The rest of the afternoon passed quickly, and before long Nancy and her friends were putting the finishing touches on their costumes. Bess helped Nancy arrange her long, reddish blond hair so that she could wear the elaborate imitation pearl-and-diamond headdress that had come with her queen's costume.

They were almost ready to leave when they heard a noise at the bottom of the stairs. Nancy looked down and jumped back in horror. She heard Ned draw his breath in.

Standing there was an imposing figure wearing a frightening bat costume. The mask was chillingly realistic.

"*Dad!*" exclaimed Brian, sounding half-embarrassed. The mask was removed to reveal the smiling face of Bartholomew Seaton.

"I guess I make a pretty convincing vampire," he said.

"You certainly do, Mr. Seaton," Bess said with a gasp. "I think you just took five years off my life."

"My apologies," Mr. Seaton said. "I wouldn't want to do that." He seemed in much better spirits than he had been a few hours earlier. "I'm leaving in a few minutes," he went on. "Brian, I'm taking the sedan. You kids can come along in the limousine when you're ready."

Mr. Seaton pulled his voluminous cape around him as he crossed the hall and swept gracefully out of the house. He was playing his role to the hilt.

After her headdress was in place, Nancy wandered downstairs. She walked slowly through the living room, the dining room, a sitting room, and the music room. Mr. Seaton seemed to like photographs as much as he liked paintings. There were framed pictures everywhere—dozens of Brian as

17

he was growing up. Nancy saw him wearing a cowboy suit and riding a pony, blowing out the candles on a birthday cake, grinning as he held up a fish he had caught, and looking solemn in a suit and tie. There were photos of Mr. Seaton, too, and several of some older people Nancy didn't know. But nowhere did she see a picture of the beautiful woman in *Danielle's Dream.*

Nancy thought about what Brian had said about his father—"He locked away every single photo of her"—and she wondered how Mrs. Seaton had died. She'd have to ask Ned, but she had a feeling he didn't know much more than she did.

Nancy's thoughts were interrupted when her friends came dashing down the stairs.

"Nancy?" Ned called. "Come on. We're ready to go!"

Nancy left her thoughts of Brian's mother behind. She ran to the front hall and joined Scarlett O'Hara, Cleopatra, Louis XVI, and Jean Laffite. The five of them piled into the limousine, and Brian pulled away from the house. "I love driving this boat," he commented. "Bosworth's off tonight."

The Silver Sail Yacht Club was a twenty-minute drive from the Seaton mansion. Brian pulled into the already crowded parking lot and found a space not too far from the club entrance.

Nancy couldn't believe her eyes when she stepped inside the ballroom. It was beautiful. Large paintings covered the walls. Each showed a different Mardi Gras scene. The tables surrounding the dance floor had been decorated to look like Mardi Gras floats. And whirling around the dance floor were people in one astounding costume after another. Three different kinds of bands were tuning up—a traditional Dixieland group, a rock band, and a large dance orchestra.

"Look at the food," Bess exclaimed. "I don't even know what some of this is, but when I get finished I'll have to diet for a month."

Nancy laughed. "Whatever happened to willpower?"

"She left it in River Heights," George replied.

"Well, I know Bess," Ned said. "And I'm not worried. If she's not sure what something is, she won't eat it."

"Then let me be your guide," said Brian. He walked up and down the tables, pointing out traditional Creole and Cajun dishes such as gumbo, which he said was a souplike stew loaded with shellfish, okra, Tabasco, and chili.

"I want to try it all," said Bess, eyeing some crayfish, another New Orleans specialty.

"Well, we can't let Bess go it alone," said George.

"Definitely not," agreed Ned.

In front of them were oysters, shrimp, cheeses, breads, and other hot dishes.

"It's a feast," said Nancy. She picked up a plate and began to serve herself.

After eating, they danced. Brian introduced them to some of his friends. Mr. Seaton came by briefly to say hello, then he moved on to talk to friends and acquaintances, all of whom complimented him on his bat costume.

Warren Tyler danced near them. He smiled

and waved to them. He was dressed like a frontiersman from the old west. His partner was wearing a clown costume.

When Bess's feet began to hurt, everyone decided to take a soda break. Brian asked if anyone had seen his father.

"I've been looking for him on and off for more than an hour," he said. "No one seems to know where he went. I even asked Warren. He hasn't seen Dad either."

"Can't help you, Brian," Ned said. "Then again, I haven't been looking for him."

The girls said the same thing. Brian asked a few of his father's friends. No one remembered seeing Bartholomew Seaton after ten o'clock. Brian shrugged it off, saying it wasn't unusual for his father to disappear like that. It usually had something to do with business.

It was about twenty minutes later that several waiters came onto the floor and began to shout:

"Is Warren Tyler here?" "Mr. Warren Tyler?" "Paging Mr. Warren Tyler!"

It took just a minute for them to find Mr. Tyler and another minute for Tyler's face to fade into deep concern. He quickly sought out Brian.

"Where's your father?" he demanded.

"I don't know. I haven't seen him," answered Brian.

Tyler looked around, almost in a panic. "Look, would you do me a favor? I don't see the people I came with. Can you drive me home? The police called to say they're headed over there. There's some kind of emergency. The burglar alarm has been set off!"

Brian looked startled. He glanced at Ned, who nodded. "Nancy and I will go with you," Ned said quickly.

Brian made arrangements for his friends to bring Bess and George home later. Then he, Nancy, Ned, and Warren Tyler jumped into the Seatons' limousine and sped away from the Silver Sail Yacht Club.

Tyler was a nervous wreck. He kept telling Brian to go faster and faster. When Brian finally pulled up in front of Tyler's house, police cars were everywhere, their red lights flashing. Police barricades were set up around the house and grounds and an ambulance was just leaving the scene. A young police officer rushed up to the limousine and demanded to know who they were.

"I'm Warren Tyler. I live here!"

He jumped out of the car, followed by the others, and ran inside. More police were in the living room. It took him just a few seconds to find that his worst fears had been realized. There was a bare spot on the wall over the marble fireplace. *Danielle's Dream* had been stolen!

3

The Prime Suspect

Warren Tyler ran to the fireplace as if he expected the painting to magically reappear. The police were going about their business—taking fingerprints, looking for clues, snapping photographs—and at first they paid no attention to Tyler's dramatic appearance. Finally, a young officer in street clothes approached him.

"Excuse me, sir, but are you Warren Tyler?" he asked politely.

"Of course I'm Warren Tyler. Who else would be so upset by this!" Tyler gestured wildly above the mantelpiece.

"Try to relax, Mr. Tyler," the police officer said. "I'm sure we'll get to the bottom of this."

"Relax!" cried Tyler. "Do you know what was taken? Do you know what all this means? What happened to my alarm system? Where are my guards?"

Instead of relaxing, Tyler was becoming increasingly upset. The young officer saw that he had better give him a few more minutes to himself. He turned to Nancy and Ned, who had come in quietly after Tyler.

"Are you with Mr. Tyler?" he asked.

"Sort of," Nancy said. "We're staying at the home of his cousin, Bartholomew Seaton. Mr. Seaton's son, Brian, is a friend of ours. He drove Mr. Tyler here and we came along. I'm Nancy Drew and this is Ned Nickerson. Brian is in the hall trying to reach his father on the phone."

"Lieutenant Mark Duford," the police officer said, shaking their hands quickly. The young officer seemed to be relieved to be talking to someone who wasn't ranting and raving. "Do you know anything about the painting that was stolen?"

"A little," said Nancy. She told him what Brian had said about *Danielle's Dream.*

"It had great sentimental value," added Ned.

The lieutenant raised his eyebrows and looked back at the fireplace. "Probably a hefty monetary value, too, if it was a Beaulieu original."

Tyler was still pacing furiously, so Lieutenant Duford turned back to Nancy and Ned.

"How did you learn about the painting?" he asked.

"We just arrived in New Orleans today," Nancy said. "Brian Seaton met us at the airport. He had to stop here to pick up his father. That's when we met Mr. Tyler and saw the painting."

"You saw the painting?"

"Yes, and it was quite impressive, though I'm no expert," Nancy said.

"And you and your friend are here for . . . ?"

23

"Just on vacation," Ned said. "We came for Mardi Gras."

Lieutenant Duford nodded. "Well, I'd better try to talk with Mr. Tyler again."

By this time Tyler was slumped in a chair holding his forehead in his right hand. He looked devastated. But when Lieutenant Duford approached him, he sat up.

"How could this happen?" he asked, speaking more quietly than he had earlier.

"Whoever did it was either very good, or very lucky," Duford replied. "The robbery took place between ten and eleven o'clock. Apparently he—or she—bypassed the alarm system on the way in, then overpowered the guard. We think the thief tripped the alarm system on the way out, but by then he probably didn't care. The guard saw nothing. All he could say were two words before he blacked out. He's on his way to the hospital now. The two words were 'The Bat.' Does that mean anything to you, Mr. Tyler?"

Tyler almost leaped to his feet. "You bet it does," he said in an excited voice. "I can tell you right now who took my painting. It was Bartholomew Seaton!"

Tyler's accusation brought a raised eyebrow from Lieutenant Duford. It also brought Ned and Nancy to attention. Nancy looked over her shoulder to make sure Brian hadn't come into the room. Too late. He was standing in the doorway with a look of both surprise and anger in his face.

"My father wouldn't do that," he said quietly.

"Oh, no?" Tyler barked, looking at Brian.

24

"Your father was at the ball tonight in a bat costume. You yourself asked me twice if I had seen him. It was after ten and he was nowhere to be found. Those kids didn't know where he was, either." Tyler pointed to Nancy and Ned, who nodded to confirm his story.

"Still, Mr. Tyler," Lieutenant Duford said, "wouldn't that be a bit obvious? After all, hundreds of people saw Seaton dressed as a bat. That would be like advertising your own crime."

"I don't care how obvious it looks. Bartholomew Seaton is a clever man. And he has his reasons."

"What do you mean by that?" asked the lieutenant.

"I'd rather not go into it now," Tyler said. "You just find Seaton and you'll find my painting. I'd bet my life on it."

Leaving his men behind to look for clues, Lieutenant Duford decided to go to the Seaton home. He asked Warren Tyler to go with him.

"That suits me fine," Brian said. He glared at Warren Tyler. "I want to see your face when you realize the mistake you've made. My father is not a thief!"

The Seaton mansion was dark when they arrived. It was the servants' night off. Brian let everyone inside.

"I told you," Warren Tyler said smugly. "He's not even here. He's probably hiding the painting somewhere."

"Calm down, Mr. Tyler," Lieutenant Duford said. "Why don't you see if you can remember anything else about the painting so I know just what I'm dealing with. Any details might be helpful."

Though still visibly upset, Tyler related some of the facts about *Danielle's Dream*. He told Lieutenant Duford what Brian had told his friends earlier—that he had found the painting several years after purchasing an abandoned farm outside the city, and that the farm had been owned by Lucien Beaulieu. Recently he'd found four Beaulieu paintings in the old barn. Three had been sold to a local gallery. Tyler had kept the portrait.

"So you're telling me that not a whole lot of people knew about *Danielle's Dream*," Lieutenant Duford said.

"That's right. And that's why I know Bartholomew Seaton is the thief."

"I'm *what*, Warren?"

The booming voice of Bartholomew Seaton carried across the large living room. Mr. Seaton looked larger than life, standing in the doorway, still wearing his bat costume from the ball. He hadn't even taken the mask off.

"You're the thief," Tyler repeated, without a pause.

"Warren, what on earth are you talking about?" Mr. Seaton asked. He removed his bat mask. "Have you gone crazy?" He suddenly noticed Lieutenant Duford. "And just who are you?" asked Brian's father haughtily.

"Lieutenant Duford, New Orleans P.D. May I ask where you've been all evening?"

26

"At the Silver Sail ball. One of the waiters gave me a message from my son to come home."

"You were not at the ball at ten o'clock. May I ask where you were, Mr. Seaton?"

Seaton shrugged. "So I left the party for a while," he said. "That's not unusual. I often leave parties for various reasons."

"I'm not interested in various reasons," the lieutenant said. "I'd just like to know where you were tonight."

"That I cannot tell you. I was engaged in a totally private business matter. With clients who insist on anonymity."

Nancy saw that the lieutenant was annoyed by Mr. Seaton's refusal to answer his questions. But before he could reply, Warren Tyler jumped in again.

"Your so-called private matter involved stealing my painting."

"What is this nonsense you keep spouting, Warren?"

"Nonsense! You call the theft of *Danielle's Dream* nonsense?"

Finally Bartholomew Seaton understood. He stepped forward until he towered over Warren Tyler. "You mean to say that someone has stolen the portrait?"

"Stop playing games, Bartholomew. You know who did it."

"No," Mr. Seaton moaned. "Not *Danielle's Dream.*"

"That's right, Mr. Seaton," Lieutenant Duford said. "So perhaps now you can see why I'd like to

27

know your whereabouts between ten o'clock and when you returned to the ball."

"I can understand that, Lieutenant," Mr. Seaton said, "but I don't understand why I'm a suspect in the first place."

"I'll tell you why!" Tyler shouted. "Because that painting means more to me than anything else! I told you I'd never sell it to you!"

"That's true," said Mr. Seaton slowly and quietly.

"So," continued Tyler, "you thought the only way to get Danielle back was to steal her!"

4

Ransom Note

"Warren, I really think you've lost your mind," Mr. Seaton said, shaking his head slowly. "I refuse to discuss this with you any further."

"Unfortunately, Mr. Seaton," Lieutenant Duford said, "you're going to have to discuss it further with me. I would appreciate it if you would come down to headquarters."

"Am I under arrest?" Mr. Seaton demanded.

"Absolutely not. But we can talk privately downtown and perhaps put some of these missing pieces together."

"Very well, Lieutenant. Maybe that's best. But I still can't tell you where I was tonight. My word means something in some circles."

"Not in mine," Warren Tyler said hotly.

Bartholomew Seaton changed his clothes, and at the lieutenant's request, turned his bat costume over to the police. He and Lieutenant Duford left in the squad car with Warren Tyler. As the car was pulling away, a bewildered George and Bess came into the house.

"What's going on?" George asked, as Ned,

Nancy, and Brian greeted them. "We just saw the police."

"It's just routine," Nancy started to say.

"Routine!" exclaimed Bess. Then she added with a sigh, "I guess I should have known we can't go anywhere with Nancy without something happening."

"It wasn't just something," Brian said. *Danielle's Dream* was stolen, and Warren is saying my father took it."

"Oh, no. That beautiful painting," cried Bess. "Brian, I can't believe your father took it."

"I can't believe it, either," Brian replied. "But I think he just might get blamed for the theft, anyway."

"What makes you think that?" Nancy asked.

"For one thing, if my father says he won't tell anyone where he was tonight, he won't tell. So there goes his alibi. For another, there are a number of people in New Orleans who would like nothing better than to see Bartholomew Seaton in a whole lot of trouble."

"Come on, Brian," Ned said calmly. "Don't you think you're exaggerating just a bit?"

Brian shook his head. "No. What I'm saying is true. My father is going to need someone on his side. I know I asked you all down here to enjoy the Mardi Gras, but now things have changed. Nancy, Ned's told me all about your detective work. Would you try to find out who really stole the painting?"

"Sure," Nancy replied. "But your father hasn't been accused of anything yet."

"Not by the police. But you heard Warren. It's pretty obvious that he'd love to see my father hurt or his reputation ruined."

"Why?" asked Nancy. Her voice took on a familiar, harder edge. Ned, Bess, and George knew all too well what that meant. She had crossed the line. She was no longer just a concerned friend. Whether she realized it or not, she was now working on the case as a detective. "Just because they were in love with the same woman?" Nancy pressed.

"Well, it's more than that," Brian said. "My dad and Warren grew up together. Their families were close, but for some reason as boys they were always competing against each other. They competed in school, in sports, for awards, you name it. And my dad always managed to come out just slightly ahead. My mother was their last great competition. Dad won, as usual. Warren has always been jealous and resentful of my father's successes."

"That's dumb," said Bess.

"Maybe," agreed Brian. "But try telling that to Warren. He's been in my father's shadow all his life. He doesn't know anything different." Brian paused for a moment. Then he said, "And he's not the only one with a grudge against Dad."

"What do you mean?" asked Nancy.

"Well, my grandfather—my mother's father, Michael Westlake—has never liked my father. Especially since the ac—since my mother died," Brian said quickly. "He's hardly spoken to him since then."

"Interesting," Nancy said. "Is your grandfather still alive?"

"Very much. In fact, I hate to say it, but he wouldn't mind seeing my father hurt, either."

"Brian," Nancy said gently, "would you mind telling me how your mother died?"

Brian drew in a deep breath. He stuck his hands in his pockets. "She was killed in a boating accident fifteen years ago. Grandfather has always blamed my dad, and he's never forgiven him. In fact, he hates him."

"I'm sorry, Brian," Nancy said, quietly.

"It must be very hard for you," Bess added. "Do you ever see your grandfather?"

"I see him when I can. He's been good to me. He loved my mother very much."

An awkward silence fell.

"Listen, Brian," Ned said after a moment. "Don't worry. If anyone can clear this thing up, Nancy can."

"I'll sure try," Nancy added.

"Nancy, I'm sorry," Brian said again. "I know you came down here for a good time, but . . ."

Nancy held up a hand. "Hey, we'll still have fun," she said. "I'll just do a little digging in between. Maybe it will turn out to be an easy one."

Brian smiled bravely, but everyone could see just how worried he was. "I'm going to bed now," he said. "Maybe a good night's sleep will help. See you in the morning."

After Brian left, the four friends sat down on sofas in the living room. It was only then that

32

they realized they were still dressed in their costumes from the ball. There they were—a Southern belle, a French king and queen, and an Egyptian queen discussing a mysterious burglary. They laughed about that for a moment. Then George asked the question they were all thinking about.

"Nan, what if Bartholomew Seaton did steal the painting?"

Nancy frowned. "The man doesn't exactly make a good first impression."

"And," Bess added, "he doesn't have an alibi. I wonder why he won't say where he was tonight."

Everyone shook their heads. Ned stood up. "I'll tell you one thing. I really don't think Brian could handle the fact that his father is a thief. Let's hope Mr. Seaton didn't do it."

"Unfortunately, he's our only suspect right now," Nancy said grimly. She then stood up as well. "I think it's time Marie Antoinette turned back into Nancy Drew and got some sleep."

The others agreed. Morning would arrive soon enough. And Nancy was no longer simply on vacation. She had a mystery to solve.

The next morning, when Nancy entered the dining room, she saw Bartholomew Seaton sitting at the table. He looked tired and not very happy. Nancy told him that Brian had asked her to work on the case. Mr. Seaton didn't say anything. He just glanced at Nancy in a way that said he didn't think much of her as a detective. That didn't surprise her. Because of her age, many people had felt that way. But it usually didn't take long for Nancy to change their minds.

"I suppose you won't tell me where you were last night," she said, as she and George joined him at the breakfast table.

"If I didn't tell the police, I'm certainly not going to tell you," Mr. Seaton replied gruffly. "What I will tell you is that I didn't take the painting. That's the truth."

"Well, it's a starting point," Nancy said. "But you were The Bat. And you did leave the ball after ten o'clock. The robbery took place between ten and eleven o'clock, according to the police."

"Purely circumstantial evidence," Mr. Seaton replied. He pushed his plate away from him. "And now, if you'll excuse me, I've got some work to do in my study. Enjoy your breakfast." He started to leave the dining room, then turned back to Nancy. "Please don't worry about this, Nancy," he said. "I'm sure it will be resolved soon."

Nancy stared after him as he headed for his study.

"Wow," said George softly.

"He's not going to make my job any easier," Nancy commented. "*That's* for sure!"

The girls finished their breakfast. Ned and Brian had gone out early. It was Ned's idea. He wanted to take Brian's mind off the events of the previous night, so he had suggested eating breakfast out and then doing some sightseeing. Nancy and George waited for Bess to come downstairs.

34

"You know something," she said, when she walked into the dining room. "As much as I enjoyed being dressed as a Southern belle, I'm definitely more comfortable in jeans."

"Even a real Southern belle would wear jeans in this day and age," George kidded. "At least some of the time."

"Right," agreed Nancy. "See? You can still be Scarlett O'Hara, only an up-to-date version."

"Sounds good to me," Bess said, picking up a glass of orange juice. "What's happening with the case?"

"Nothing yet," replied Nancy. "The police let Mr. Seaton go. Maybe today I can start making some sense of things."

"You will," Bess assured her.

The words had no sooner left her mouth than someone began banging violently on the front door. The banging was so loud and went on for so long that Nancy jumped up and headed for the front door. But Bartholomew Seaton had reached it first. Nancy ducked back into the dining room. Bess and George hovered behind her. When Mr. Seaton opened the door the girls heard Warren Tyler's voice. He was once again accusing Brian's father of taking the portrait.

"Warren, if you've come here to act like a raving lunatic again, you're wasting your time," Mr. Seaton said loudly. "The police don't think I did it, and I don't think you really believe I did, either."

As Tyler followed Mr. Seaton into the hall, Nancy stepped out of the dining room in full view of both men. They didn't seem to care that she was watching them. Warren Tyler looked even more tired than Mr. Seaton. Nancy could see that losing the painting had hurt him deeply. She could also tell he was still convinced that Bartholomew Seaton was the thief.

"You might be fooling the police and everyone else around here, Bartholomew," Warren Tyler said, "but you won't fool me. I know your tricks. I know what you'll do when you want something. And I know you don't care who you hurt. But this time you've gone too far. I'll see you rot in jail before I'm through."

Mr. Seaton smiled patiently. "You know, Warren, sometimes I think you're losing your mind. Maybe once you find the painting you ought to take a long vacation."

"Find my painting . . . find Danielle. Ha! That's a laugh. You've made it next to impossible."

Mr. Seaton looked puzzled. Tyler fumbled in his pocket and took out an envelope. He handed it to Brian's father.

"What's this?" Mr. Seaton asked.

"You ought to know. You wrote it."

"Warren . . ." Mr. Seaton said as he opened the envelope. He looked at the contents. Then he looked at his cousin. "You think *I* wrote this?"

"Or had it written."

Mr. Seaton turned red with anger. For a second, Nancy thought he was going to punch Warren Tyler. Instead, he whirled around to face Nancy.

"Here, you look at this," he snapped. "Mr.

36

Tyler thinks I wrote it. You're a detective. What do you think?"

Nancy calmly took the note and read it aloud.

"'It will cost you one million dollars to get your painting back. Get the money fast. You will receive further instructions shortly. If you fail to do this or if you involve the police, the painting will be destroyed.'"

5

An Eerie Discovery

"Do you really think I would destroy the portrait?" Mr. Seaton asked, still looking at Nancy.

"No," she replied honestly.

It was Tyler's turn to talk to Nancy. "Where am I going to get a million dollars?" he asked bitterly. "I don't have that kind of money, certainly not in cash that I can put my hands on quickly."

"I think you should go to the police," replied Nancy. Both men were using her as a sounding board and she was trying to calm things down.

"But the note says—"

"Most ransom notes say that," Nancy interrupted. "Anyway, it's too late. The police already know the painting's been stolen, and I'm sure Lieutenant Duford won't be too surprised by a ransom demand. Besides, if the note really is from the thief, he obviously wants money, not the painting. That means the portrait is probably still in the area. The police are your best chance for getting it back."

"I don't know," Tyler said, folding the note

and placing it back in the envelope. "Getting that painting back means everything to me. It's my only—"

He stopped abruptly, not finishing the sentence. Taking a deep breath he turned back to Mr. Seaton. Brian's father glared at him.

"So you didn't take the painting," Tyler said. "All right, prove it. I can't raise this kind of money, but you can. If you didn't take *Danielle's Dream*, then help me get it back."

"You're asking an awful lot," Mr. Seaton said. "First of all, I'll need help in getting so much cash quickly. Second, you've been telling everyone I'm a thief. And third, I don't have to prove anything to you." He paused. "This is something I've got to think about. Maybe you should take Nancy's advice and go to the police."

Tyler's anger began mounting again. But he managed to control himself. He nodded abruptly, turned on his heel, and left the house.

"Thanks for stepping in," Mr. Seaton said to Nancy. "I really don't want to be alone with that man. He's too unstable."

"Well, Brian did ask me to look into the theft of the painting. He doesn't want you accused of something you didn't do."

"Brian's a good son," Mr. Seaton said. He smiled briefly. Then he returned to his study, and Nancy walked back to the dining room where Bess was now finishing her breakfast. Nancy had a feeling the case was going to be tougher than she first thought. There was still a great deal she didn't know.

She wondered if Tyler would take the ransom

39

note to the police or try to go it alone. Since he didn't have a solid promise from Mr. Seaton, he would probably go to the police to cover all the bases. The man was definitely unnerved.

When Bess had finished her breakfast, the girls tried to decide what to do. They didn't know how long Ned and Brian would be gone. George suggested that they call a cab and go downtown and see some of the sights.

Fifteen minutes later the doorbell rang. Thinking their cab had arrived, Nancy went to the door—and found herself facing a short, stout, balding man, with a small mustache and round eyeglasses.

"Hello," Nancy said. "I—"

"Where's that scoundrel Seaton?" was the man's greeting. "I know he's here. I demand to see him."

"Just a moment," Nancy said politely. "Whom shall I say is calling?"

"Ferdinand Koch," the man said angrily. "And believe me, he'll know what this is about."

At that moment a taxi pulled up to the house. Nancy told the driver to wait, then headed for Mr. Seaton's study. On the way, she met Bess and George.

"The taxi's here," she said, "but I can't go with you right now."

"Why not?" George asked.

"What's going on?" echoed Bess.

"There's a man here to see Mr. Seaton. His name is Koch. He must be the art dealer Brian mentioned. I'd better hang around."

"Then we won't go, either," said George.

40

"No, you two go," Nancy said. "We came down here to have fun. It's not your fault I got involved in a case."

Bess and George looked at each other. They knew there was no sense arguing with Nancy Drew when she was working.

"All right, you win," George said. "But we'll try to call you later. Maybe you can meet us somewhere this afternoon."

"Sounds good to me," Nancy said. "Now get going and remember everything you see, so you can tell me all about it."

The two girls brushed past the impatient Mr. Koch and left. Then Nancy headed for Mr. Seaton's study and knocked on the door.

"Come in," Mr. Seaton said.

Nancy entered. Bartholomew Seaton was seated behind an old oak desk, looking over some papers. The floor was covered by a thick, rust-colored carpet and there were built-in oak bookshelves along two walls. Along another wall were a large computer, a photocopy machine, and a telex machine. Nancy could see that a great deal of business took place from this office.

"There's a man here to see you," she said. "A Mr. Ferdinand Koch."

Brian's father nodded. "Old Ferdinand, eh. Right on schedule. Come with me, Nancy," he said. "I think you'll find this interesting."

Nancy accompanied Mr. Seaton to the door, well aware that his attitude toward her was changing. She couldn't help wondering why. Did he really think she could help him? Or was he a clever criminal attempting to lull her into think-

41

ing he was an innocent victim? She knew she couldn't let down her guard.

"Ferdinand, come in," Mr. Seaton said. "I'd offer you a cup of coffee, but something tells me this isn't a social call."

Mr. Koch stepped into the foyer.

"You certainly didn't waste any time, did you, Seaton?" he said, wiping his forehead.

"I never waste time," Mr. Seaton answered. "So please get to the point, Ferdinand."

"*Danielle's Dream*. Where is it? What have you done with it?"

Bartholomew Seaton shook his head. "You, too? Well, it shouldn't surprise me. I seem to be everyone's favorite target lately."

"What makes you think you can get away with something like this?" Koch asked. "One of these days you'll fall. Underhanded businessmen like you always fall sooner or later."

"You know, Ferdinand, you're so excited that you've lost your manners. There's a young lady standing here and you haven't given me a chance to introduce her. Nancy Drew, this is Ferdinand Koch, owner of the very prestigious Koch Gallery and one of New Orleans's best-known art dealers and collectors."

Mr. Koch made a face. "I didn't know you introduced your housekeepers, Seaton," he said.

Mr. Seaton smiled. "You know what I like about you, Ferdinand? You're rarely right. Nancy is a friend of my son's. She's visiting the Mardi Gras. But she also happens to be a detective. Brian has asked her to find out who *really* stole the painting."

42

Koch looked at Nancy and raised his eyebrows. "A detective?"

"That's right, Mr. Koch," Nancy said. "Would you mind telling me your interest in *Danielle's Dream?* I thought it belonged to Warren Tyler."

"My gallery," said Koch, standing as tall as he was able, "is well known the world over. We try to acquire as many pieces of fine art as we can. I bought the other Beaulieu paintings that Tyler found, and I was going to acquire *Danielle's Dream,* too, despite the fact that the style seems a bit unusual for Beaulieu. At least, I *was* going to acquire it. Now it's disappeared."

Koch's statement surprised Nancy. Warren Tyler had said he wouldn't sell the painting. He'd made that quite clear. Now Nancy had to look at things in a new light.

"Don't pay any attention to Ferdinand," Mr. Seaton said quickly. "He thinks he can buy things that aren't even for sale."

"At least I buy them, I don't steal them," Koch replied.

"I think I've heard about enough, Ferdinand," Mr. Seaton said. "You've had your fun. Now I think you'd better leave."

"With pleasure. But you haven't seen the last of me, Seaton." With that, Koch turned and marched out of the house.

When Koch was gone, Brian's father turned to Nancy. "You can see what I'm up against."

"Yes, but tell me, Mr. Seaton, was Warren Tyler planning to sell *Danielle's Dream?*"

Mr. Seaton shrugged. "You never know with Warren. I doubt it. But I think Koch convinced

43

himself that he could talk Warren into selling. *Danielle's Dream* would be a wonderful addition to his gallery. It would command a lot of local attention."

Nancy nodded.

"Well," Mr. Seaton said, "if you'll excuse me, I have to make a few phone calls."

He returned to his study, and Nancy returned to the living room. Why were both Warren Tyler and Ferdinand Koch so positive that Bartholomew Seaton was the thief? she wondered. And if he were the thief, what would Mr. Seaton have to gain? Money? He seemed to have plenty of that. And he couldn't hang a stolen painting over his mantel. Then again, some people liked to possess things just for the sake of possessing them, even if they had to be hidden. Maybe that's the way it was with *Danielle's Dream.* Mr. Seaton didn't want a valuable painting. He just wanted a memory of his wife.

Nancy's thoughts were interrupted when Brian and Ned returned home.

"Hi!" she said, cheerfully.

"Hi," Ned answered. "Where are Bess and George? We left so early we began to feel guilty about deserting you."

"They're downtown, sightseeing."

"What are you up to?" Ned asked.

"I stayed behind to do a little investigating," Nancy said. "Ferdinand Koch was here this morning. So was Mr. Tyler."

"I told you she wouldn't waste any time," Ned said to Brian. "She'll find out who took the painting."

44

"Mr. Tyler received a ransom note," Nancy told them. "Whoever took the painting wants one million dollars for its return."

"A million!" Ned gasped. "I didn't think it was worth that much. Beaulieu was just a local artist."

"I know," Nancy said thoughtfully. "It's odd."

"Look," Brian said. "I feel terrible for ruining your vacation. Tonight all of us are going out on the town. My treat. And I don't want to hear any argument."

Nancy smiled. "You've got yourself a deal."

That afternoon, Nancy, Ned, and Brian decided to take a dip in the heated pool. They swam, lounged around, and challenged each other to races. It was a good way to forget about the case for a while.

Bess and George returned around four, carrying souvenirs and complaining about aching feet. But they had had a good time, and when they heard they'd all be going out again that night, they were all for it. They didn't even want to rest.

After dinner, at eight o'clock, Nancy and the others headed downtown in Brian's sedan. They parked near the French Quarter, one of the oldest sections of the city, and began walking.

People were crowded everywhere, but they all seemed happy and friendly. Dixieland music blared from the cafés, and some people were dancing on the sidewalks.

Street musicians and artists were on almost every corner and many people were in costume. Nancy saw everything from colorful clowns to ghosts and witches. She also noticed the perfect-ly preserved old houses that could only be found in the French Quarter of New Orleans.

Bess and George had totally forgotten about their aching feet of the afternoon, and Nancy knew they were having a good time. Even Brian was laughing and enjoying himself. He seemed to have let go of the problems his father was having. At least for the time being.

"We've got to come back for the big parade so you can see all the floats," Brian said enthusiasti-cally. "And I want to take you for a cruise on the *Natchez*. You'll love it."

"What's the *Natchez?*" Bess asked.

"A restored paddle wheeler," Brian answered. "Just like the boats that used to take people up and down the Mississippi years ago. It's got a huge wooden paddle wheel in the rear that drives the boat. It's another New Orleans tradi-tion."

"Sounds like fun," George said.

"Yes, if nothing interferes with it," Bess added, looking directly at Nancy.

"Okay, okay," Nancy said. "I promise I won't spoil anyone's fun. We'll work something out."

"The famous last words of Nancy Drew," Ned remarked. He nudged Nancy on the shoulder. "You watch, before this night is out something will happen to bring Nancy right back to this case."

"Not this time," Bess said. "Not tonight."

But Nancy didn't hear Bess's words. She'd stopped cold in her tracks, her eyes riveted to the crowd down the street. Ned turned and saw her

46

staring. But before he could speak, Nancy plunged into the crowd away from her friends. She was trying frantically to reach something—or someone.

"Nancy!" Ned hollered, but she acted as if she hadn't heard him. His shout caught the attention of the others though, and in a flash they were all dashing after her.

Nancy ran madly, shoving people aside as she battled her way through the crowd. Finally she slowed down. After another moment, she stopped and leaned up against a streetlight. She was breathing heavily.

Ned was the first to reach her.

"What in the world made you run off like that?" he exclaimed. Then he looked at her more closely. "Nancy? Are you all right? You look as if you've seen a ghost."

"Maybe I have," she said, still gasping for breath. "I know it sounds crazy, but I just saw Danielle Seaton—or someone who looks exactly like the woman in the painting!"

6

Michael Westlake

Nancy was very upset. So was Brian. The others tried to assure them that it was some kind of mistake. The five of them went dancing for a while, but it was no use. They just couldn't enjoy themselves.

Finally they headed for home, much earlier than they had planned.

"I can't get her face out of my mind," Nancy said, over a cup of hot tea. "I just caught a glimpse of her in the crowd, but she looked exactly like the woman in the painting."

"My mother," Brian said slowly.

"Well, it's got to be some kind of coincidence," Bess said. "What else could it be?"

"I don't know," Nancy said. "I remember how I felt when I saw the painting at Mr. Tyler's house. That face did something to me. I've been thinking about it ever since we saw it. And that woman tonight. It was . . . her."

"Nancy," Brian said. "There is no way my mother is still alive. Believe me."

"Maybe," George suggested, "the face in the

painting made such an impression on you that it sort of burned into your mind. Then when you saw someone who resembled Brian's mother in the painting, well, your imagination took over."

"I can't explain it," Nancy said. "I really can't."

"Maybe it was some relative of yours," Bess said to Brian.

Brian shook his head. "I can't think of anyone who looks like that—like my mother."

"Well, all I know is that it was a frightening experience," Nancy said. "Really frightening."

"You don't have to convince me," Ned said. "When I reached you at the lamppost, you're the one who looked like a ghost. Your face was white as a sheet."

"This is all my fault," Brian said. "I never should have asked you to take this case."

"Don't be silly," Nancy said. "Even if the painting hadn't been stolen I would have seen that woman and had the same reaction. It has nothing to do with the case."

But did it? That's what Nancy was really wondering. What were the details of the boating accident that had killed Mrs. Seaton? Brian hadn't been specific. *Could* the woman have been Brian's mother? The others kept saying Nancy's imagination was at fault, that the woman was a look-alike, or a distant relative. After all, Brian might not know *all* his relatives, especially on his mother's side of the family. But Nancy was skeptical. Nancy had been a detective long enough to trust her senses. When something such as this happened, no matter how unlikely or crazy, she had to follow up on it. She couldn't afford to dismiss anything that might be connected to the case.

Nancy didn't sleep well that night. She kept dreaming and waking up. When she would fall back asleep, she'd dream again. Always the same thing. The woman's face. If for no other reason, she wanted to find the painting just to see that face again. Nancy decided she would have to pick up the pace of her investigation. Mardi Gras and her vacation would have to take a backseat.

The next morning, Nancy decided to pay a visit to Michael Westlake, Brian's grandfather, who was the owner of a large, import-export business in the city. When she arrived at his office she told a secretary that she was a friend of Brian Seaton's and wanted to talk to Mr. Westlake about a family matter. Nancy waited in the outer office. After several minutes, the secretary showed her into Michael Westlake's office.

"Come in, Ms. Drew," Mr. Westlake said, rising from his chair behind an antique desk. "I've got a busy schedule this morning, but I always have time for a friend of Brian's. How may I help you? You said it involves a family matter, didn't you?"

Michael Westlake was a tall, distinguished-looking man in his early sixties. He had black hair that was peppered with white. His dark eyes reminded Nancy of Danielle's eyes in the portrait.

50

"How long have you known Brian?" he asked, as he indicated a comfortable chair in front of his desk.

"Well, I actually met him two days ago," said Nancy. Mr. Westlake looked puzzled, so she continued. "Brian invited his college friend Ned Nickerson down for Mardi Gras. Ned's a friend of mine, and Brian was nice enough to let Ned bring a few of *his* friends along."

"I see. But what kind of family matter could you possibly want to discuss with me?"

Nancy then told him about the theft of the painting and the accusations made against Bartholomew Seaton. Michael Westlake apparently knew nothing about the matter. But as soon as he heard the name Bartholomew Seaton, his face began to turn red.

"It wouldn't surprise me if Bartholomew *was* behind it," he said. "That man will do anything to get what he wants."

Nancy cleared her throat. "Brian told me that you and Mr. Seaton haven't spoken for quite some time."

"That's personal," Mr. Westlake said, with a touch of annoyance in his voice. "And I still can't understand why you're here."

"I'm here because Brian asked me to investigate the theft of the painting. No matter what your feelings are for Mr. Seaton, he's still Brian's father, and Brian doesn't want to see him accused of something he didn't do."

"Brian asked *you* to investigate the theft?" Mr. Westlake looked at Nancy skeptically.

Nancy expected him to order her out of his office. Instead, he stood up and walked toward the window.

"I love Brian," he said as he stared out the window. "He's my daughter's only child." He turned around and faced Nancy again. "But his father was responsible for Danielle's death. No one will convince me otherwise. My daughter died in a boating accident. From everything I've learned, she could have been saved if Seaton hadn't been so careless."

"I'm sorry," Nancy said. "I didn't know that about Mr. Seaton."

"Maybe Brian forgives more easily than I do," Mr. Westlake said. "And as far as this painting you mentioned is concerned, I know nothing about it. But if Warren Tyler and Ferdinand Koch think Bartholomew took it, I'd bet they're right."

"Do you know Mr. Tyler and Mr. Koch?"

"Yes, I do. Through my business," Westlake replied.

"Let me ask you something," Nancy said. "Can you think of any reason why Mr. Seaton would want a painting he couldn't display?"

Mr. Westlake snorted. "Sure. Seaton's greedy and selfish. He takes things just because he knows other people want them. He'd steal the painting so Tyler couldn't have it, even if he didn't want the painting himself. You know, I don't think he ever even loved my Danielle. He just wanted her so Tyler couldn't marry her. Now he's keeping her from him again. He's not a sentimental man. The portrait wouldn't hold any meaning for him."

Nancy frowned. "Are you sure? Brian said that after your daughter's death Mr. Seaton couldn't bear to look at photos of her. He had to lock them away. That sounds sentimental to me."

"Sentimental? That's ridiculous! Seaton was glad she was gone. He knew he'd made a mistake in marrying her. He just wanted to get rid of the evidence, as they say, so he could start over again."

"But he never remarried," Nancy pointed out.

"True," replied Mr. Westlake, looking uncomfortable. "That doesn't mean he hasn't had girl-friends, though."

"Maybe he's changed," suggested Nancy.

"Seaton," said Mr. Westlake, "is a snake. He might shed a layer of skin, but he'll never change."

Michael Westlake walked back to his desk, sat down, and began to look through some papers. It was clear to Nancy that the interview was over. She stood up. But when she reached the door, Mr. Westlake called her back.

"I have just one more thing to say about Bartholomew Seaton," he said, his voice choked with anger. "If I weren't a civilized man, I'd kill him!"

7

A Close Call

Nancy drew a deep breath as she left Michael Westlake's office. She wondered if he was involved in the case. He certainly hated Bartholomew Seaton. Did he hate him enough to frame him for a crime?

From Westlake's, Nancy went to police headquarters. It was time to talk to Lieutenant Duford. If the police had any leads, she hoped he would tell her. Nancy found the lieutenant in his office. She explained that she was a detective and that Brian had asked her to investigate the case.

"So you're finding out that Bartholomew Seaton isn't exactly Mr. Popularity around here," Lieutenant Duford said, after Nancy had filled him in on her investigation.

Nancy nodded. "Does he have any sort of police record?" she asked.

"Not really. There were some negligence charges brought against him over the death of his wife, but they were dropped. There wasn't enough evidence for a conviction."

"What does Mr. Seaton do?" Nancy asked. "Brian has never been very specific about that with Ned."

"Well, mostly he's independently wealthy. But he's been very successful in a variety of businesses. For the past few years, he's been an investment consultant to businesses and individual investors. And everything he touches turns to gold—for his clients and himself."

Nancy nodded thoughtfully. She was glad the lieutenant was being so open with her.

"Did Warren Tyler show you the ransom note?" she asked suddenly.

"Yes. He turned it over to us. He's very nervous about getting the painting back."

"Would he pay the ransom?" asked Nancy.

"Sure, if someone could help him come up with the cash," Lieutenant Duford replied. "There doesn't seem to be any way he can raise that kind of money himself. Not unless he sells off stocks, businesses, the works. By the way, there's something else. Something that isn't going to make this case any easier."

"What's that?" Nancy asked, her curiosity rising.

"Well, I just got back from a meeting with Ferdinand Koch. It seems that the three Beaulieu street scenes found in Tyler's barn may not be Beaulieus after all."

"*Not* Beaulieus?" Nancy exclaimed.

"Koch has some doubts about the paintings now," said Lieutenant Duford.

But that was all the lieutenant would tell her,

55

and Nancy left the police station more puzzled than ever. The case was complicated all right.

Danielle's Dream was missing, and any of several people could be responsible. Brian's father was the obvious suspect, of course. He wanted the painting badly, and all the circumstantial evidence pointed to him. Furthermore, he knew that Tyler would never give him or even sell him the painting. Had he stolen it as a last resort? Was the ransom note a blind to put everyone off the track? If so, it wasn't working.

Neither Westlake nor Tyler was as strongly suspect as Mr. Seaton was—after all, the painting *belonged* to Tyler, and Westlake and Tyler were business acquaintances. But both of them hated Mr. Seaton. Either might have wanted to frame him for a crime.

Then there was Ferdinand Koch. He certainly wanted the painting. But would he risk his reputation and his business to steal it?

Nancy stopped in a small sandwich shop for a bite of lunch: a sandwich and a soda. She needed to think. Outside, a number of people were singing along with a couple of street musicians. But Nancy wasn't paying much attention. Other things were in her head—the theft, the haunting face of the woman, the hatred people felt for Bartholomew Seaton. Nancy finished her lunch and called Ned. She reached Bosworth, who told her the others were swimming. She left a message saying that she'd be back in a couple of hours, then went on to the Koch Gallery.

The gallery occupied an entire city block in a magnificent stone building that dated back to the turn of the century. American, French, and Spanish flags flew outside, and two imposing statues sat on each side of the front steps. Nancy quickly mounted them and went inside. The gallery was arranged like a museum and was hushed, almost silent. A number of visitors were looking quietly at the exhibits, despite the frenzy of the Mardi Gras celebration outside.

Nancy couldn't believe the wide variety of works on display. She wandered around for several minutes, then asked a security guard where Koch's office was located. When she knocked on the door, a secretary showed her inside. Ferdinand Koch looked surprised to see her. But he seemed a lot calmer than he had been at the Seaton mansion.

"I didn't expect to see you again so soon, Ms. Drew," he said.

"I'd appreciate it if you could give me a few minutes of your time," Nancy said, with a smile.

"Ah, yes, the detective." Koch sounded more amused than rude.

"By the way," Nancy said casually. "Do you know Michael Westlake?"

"Of course. He's a business associate of mine," Koch replied. "And we see each other socially from time to time."

Nancy nodded. "Well," she said, "actually, I came by to see the Beaulieu street scenes. I was just talking to Lieutenant Duford and he told me that you doubted they were authentic."

Koch nodded. "That's right. I have to have them examined by experts, of course, in order to be sure. But I'm beginning to have my doubts

that they are Beaulieus. If *Danielle's Dream* is
found and is judged an original, it becomes very
valuable," he added. "And the collection becomes even more valuable. This is especially true
because Lucien Beaulieu is dead and so can no
longer produce new paintings. It's my belief that
the artist never worked outside New Orleans, so
his works certainly belong here."

"In the Koch Gallery?"

"I can't think of a better place," Koch said,
smiling.

"But Tyler has told you he won't sell *Danielle's
Dream*," said Nancy.

Koch nodded. "He's told me that. And my
financial adviser has advised me to bid all-out for
it. He knows I would never give it up if I got my
hands on it. And Warren Tyler *will* sell it to me."

"Only if he *has* it," Nancy added.

"Obviously. But I think Seaton will come to his
senses. He certainly can't display the painting,
and I don't think he stole it to sell it. The ransom
note was just his little joke. My guess is that he
acted impulsively. He'll see his mistake, and the
painting will suddenly turn up."

"Let's hope you're right, Mr. Koch," Nancy
said. "But what if Mr. Seaton didn't steal it, and
what if someone destroys it?"

"That, my dear, would be a real tragedy."

"Mr. Koch, tell me why you doubt these
Beaulieus. What makes you want to have them
checked?"

"Several things," Koch replied. "And all of
them are clues, but none of them indicates defini-
tively that the paintings are not the work of

Lucien Beaulieu. That's why I'm bringing experts in, although the experts themselves may not have an easy time of it. You see, it isn't uncommon for an artist to change his or her style, so differences in the artwork might indicate a forgery—or they might not. But I'll tell you why I'm suspicious."

Nancy took a pad of paper and a pen out of her purse and began to make notes.

"The first clue—I mean the one that was noticed first," Koch said, "and the one that made me look closer, is the brush strokes. Beaulieu is known for his short, choppy strokes. They show up best in his oil paintings. But the strokes in the three new street scenes are more flowing than usual."

"Not like the Beaulieu style?" Nancy asked, writing down the information.

"Not really," Koch admitted. "But that doesn't necessarily mean anything. Maybe he was experimenting, trying different techniques. The paintings were hidden away, after all. It's possible he didn't like his new work but couldn't quite bear to throw it out, so he just put it where he couldn't see it. Who knows?"

"But there's more?" Nancy prompted.

"Yes. If the brush strokes had been the only thing out of the ordinary, I might have overlooked the whole business. In fact, the variation from the usual Beaulieu style might have made the paintings more valuable. But after the brush strokes were pointed out to me, I began to look more closely at the paintings. And then I noticed the artist's signature."

"His signature?" Nancy asked.

"Yes. Beaulieu usually signed his paintings at the top of the canvas rather than at the bottom. And after his signature he always noted the year the painting was completed. You know, Lucien Beaulieu, nineteen forty-six or something."

"I see," murmured Nancy.

"But these were undated, and all three were signed in the lower right-hand corner." Koch paused and rubbed his eyes tiredly. "The thing is, he didn't *always* sign his canvases at the top, and maybe there was a reason he didn't date these three. Especially if he wasn't pleased with his work.

"I have to admit, though," Koch continued, "that once I'd noticed the signature and the missing dates, I was pretty curious. So this morning I took one of the paintings out of the display myself, removed the frame, and looked at the canvas. As I was beginning to fear, I found that the canvas had been purchased at a store. It had been prestretched and was stapled onto the wood frame underneath."

Nancy looked up, frowning. "Beaulieu wouldn't have gotten his canvases from a store?" she asked.

"No," replied Koch. "He was an old-timer. He liked to stretch his canvases himself. And he attached them to the frame structure with hobnails, not a staple gun.

"After I saw the canvas," Koch went on, "I sat back and just gazed at the painting. That was when I noticed the final clue. Beaulieu always used cerulean blue in his skies. As far as I could tell, there wasn't a trace of that color in the painting I was looking at. I couldn't see any in the other street scenes either. But—once again—these clues don't mean much."

"Not separately," Nancy replied, "but all together, they add up to quite a bit of doubt."

"That's all it is, though," Koch said. "Doubt. Nothing concrete. That's why I want an expert to see the paintings. They could very well be the result of a whim, of Beaulieu trying something new, especially if they were done near the end of his career. But I'm rather, um, desperate to see *Danielle's Dream* now."

Just how desperate, are you, Mr. Koch? Nancy wondered. Desperate enough to steal the painting so you can examine it before you make one of the biggest mistakes of your career?

Nancy put her notebook away and got to her feet. She thanked Mr. Koch for his help and then wandered thoughtfully out of his office. Before she left the gallery, she stopped to look at the three Beaulieu street scenes. Just as Koch had said, they were signed at the bottom and undated, but Nancy didn't know much about brush strokes or techniques or the use of color. She had to take Koch's word on his findings.

By now it was midafternoon. Nancy wondered what her friends were doing. She wanted to return to the Seaton mansion to find out, but she had to make one last stop. She spotted a phone booth on the corner, with a phone book attached. She leafed through the pages until she found Warren Tyler's name. Under Tyler's home ad-

61

dress was the address of his office. Nancy looked at her city map and saw that the office was just a few blocks away.

At first, Warren Tyler refused to see Nancy, but when she insisted, he finally agreed.

"Well, Nancy," he said, ushering her into his office, a slight smirk on his face. "If you're here to plead Seaton's case, forget it. That man will pay for what he's done."

"Why are you so convinced that he took your painting, Mr. Tyler?" asked Nancy.

Warren Tyler gave a short laugh. "Don't judge a book by its cover, Nancy. Bartholomew Seaton can be charming. He's an actor. But he's also a fraud. There are a number of reasons he might steal it, not the least of which is his dislike for me. He's wanted everything I've ever wanted— and he's gotten it, too. He knew I wouldn't sell him *Danielle's Dream,* so he was forced to take it."

"What about the ransom note?" asked Nancy.

"Oh, that's just to throw us off the trail."

"Yet you're willing to try and pay off the ransom?"

"Yes, if it'll get my painting back," Tyler replied. "I'd do just about anything for Danielle's portrait."

"You found the paintings in an abandoned barn," Nancy said, changing the subject. "Were you looking for them? Did you know that Lucien Beaulieu had once lived and worked there?"

"I knew he'd lived there," Tyler replied. "Danielle used to take art lessons from him."

"Brian's mother took art lessons from Lucien Beaulieu?" Nancy asked, surprised.

"Yes. Anyway, I bought the property with the idea of reselling it to make a profit. One day, I was out there looking things over, and I came across the paintings. Four of them. I turned them over to the experts. That's when I learned how valuable they could be."

"Mr. Tyler, would you mind if I went out and looked at the barn, the one where you found the paintings?" asked Nancy.

"Why?" Tyler said, narrowing his eyes.

"Just curiosity," Nancy replied. "The more I know about this business, the more I might be able to help."

"Help who, Bartholomew Seaton?"

"I want to help get to the bottom of the mystery—get your painting back," countered Nancy.

"But are you working for Seaton, Nancy?" Tyler pressed.

"No, for his son. Brian doesn't think his father took *Danielle's Dream.*" Nancy paused. "Could I see the barn?" she asked again.

Tyler thought for a minute. Finally he nodded. "All right, but I'll go with you."

"When?"

"Not today," Tyler said. "I've got an important meeting in about an hour."

"Look, Mr. Tyler. This is important. I'd really like to go today. I just want to see the place. Maybe it will give me a better feel for the case."

Tyler looked at Nancy thoughtfully. Then he

63

said, "Well, all right, but be careful out there. The place is old. I wouldn't want to see you get hurt." He told her how to get out to the farm and then abruptly showed her out of his office.

It was late afternoon by the time Nancy returned to the Seaton mansion. After filling Brian and the others in on her investigation, she asked Ned to drive her out to Tyler's property. Bartholomew Seaton owned a four-wheel drive jeep, which Brian said they could use.

The Tyler property was a half-hour drive from the city. As Nancy and Ned drove along they could see that what used to be exclusively farm country was now being heavily developed, so Tyler's story about the farm being a real-estate investment could easily be true.

"What a mystery," Nancy said to Ned as they looked for the turnoff onto the dirt road that would take them to the farm. "My instincts tell me that Mr. Seaton didn't steal the painting. On the surface, he'd have nothing to gain. But everything points to him."

"What do you mean, 'on the surface'?" Ned asked.

"Well, he couldn't display a painting he had stolen," she answered. "And he doesn't seem to need the ransom money. It might just be a matter of a few people disliking Mr. Seaton for personal reasons, so naturally they point the finger at him. But then there's the thief in the bat costume, and Mr. Seaton's disappearance the night of the robbery."

"I see what you mean," Ned replied. "And the police obviously have no proof of anything yet."

Nancy shook her head. "No. Whoever took the painting left nothing behind. The only clue is the bat costume, but as Lieutenant Duford said, wearing the costume would almost be advertising the crime." She added, "There's another twist, too."

"What's that?"

Nancy told Ned about her conversation with Ferdinand Koch. "Koch has no proof," she said. "He's just a little unsure about those other paintings."

"And you thought this wouldn't be a tough one," Ned said.

"I should have known better. Hey, here we are."

Ned had been driving up a dirt road for about two miles. Tyler had told Nancy to look for a sign. The sign directed them to turn into what appeared to be a long driveway. At last, they reached the old farm.

The buildings were all weathered. Some of them were nearly crumbling. There was nothing growing on the baked-hard red clay soil. If Tyler was going to fix the farm up, he had his work cut out for him.

"Look at this place," Ned remarked. "It needs a lot of work. You couldn't farm it right now if you wanted to. I see the barn," he added, pointing to a broken-down structure off to the right. The barn siding was weathered and coming apart. The roof was almost bare of shingles and sunken in the middle. The large sliding door was in pieces on the ground. It looked as if a strong wind would collapse the building easily.

"It's hard to tell—as dilapidated as this place looks now—" Nancy said, "but I think the barn is the one in the background of *Danielle's Dream*."

Ned frowned. "Maybe you're right."

"The barn looks a little shaky," Nancy said, "but we've got to go inside."

"Then let's go," Ned answered firmly. But before he got out of the jeep, he reached into the glove compartment and pulled out a flashlight. "I thought this might come in handy," he said, showing it to Nancy.

"Good thinking," Nancy said approvingly.

The inside of the barn was as dilapidated as the outside. Most of the boards of the stalls were rotten, loose, or torn off. Ned and Nancy had to step carefully to avoid rusty nails. Rotted hay was matted on the floor and a damp, musty smell hung in the air.

"I can think of better places for a major art discovery," Ned remarked grimly.

"Me, too," Nancy said, as she wandered from stall to stall. At one, she stopped to move some fallen boards aside. She looked into the stall and found more broken boards in the back. Behind them appeared to be a crawl space. Perhaps it was the place where Tyler had found *Danielle's Dream* and the other Beaulieu paintings. She began picking her way carefully through the debris.

Nancy bent over to move a thick board. As she did, she heard a rustling noise from the loft above her. She backed away from the crawl space and looked up—and saw two huge, heavy bales of hay tumbling from the loft. They were going to land right on her head!

8

Winged Terror

Before she could react, Nancy felt something hit her, hard. Was it the tumbling bales? She rolled over, trembling. Someone was on the floor beside her. Ned! He had shoved her out of the way at the last instant with a flying tackle.

"Nancy, are you all right?" he asked anxiously.

"Yes," she replied, her heart pounding. "Oh, Ned. I thought it was all over this time."

"That was a close one," he agreed. "I hope I didn't hurt you."

"I'm fine," Nancy reassured him. She looked at the huge bales resting on the exact spot where she had stood a moment earlier. "I would have been crushed by those things if you hadn't acted so fast," she said.

"Football training," Ned kidded. "Easiest tackle I ever made." Then, after a pause, he added, "Do you want to head back to Brian's?"

Nancy started to nod in agreement, but she suddenly stopped. Her fright was slowly turning to anger.

"If we leave now," she said, "we won't have

learned anything. I want to look behind that stall. And there's something else we haven't thought about."

"What's that?" Ned asked.

"What if it wasn't an accident? What if somebody was in that loft? Maybe somebody doesn't want us poking around out here."

"It's a possibility," he said.

"We have to find out," Nancy said. "I want to take a look around up there."

"Well, what are we waiting for?" replied Ned.

They got up and brushed themselves off. When Nancy looked back up at the loft she felt a shudder go through her. Then she took a deep breath and turned to Ned.

"Okay. Let's find a way to get up there," she said.

Within minutes, they had fashioned a make-shift ladder from some boards and the two bales of hay. Ned climbed up first, with Nancy right behind him. The loft was dark and musty, and the old boards creaked.

"We need more light," Nancy said. "The flashlight isn't enough. Can you make it to the end of the loft and open the doors?"

"I think so," Ned answered.

He crawled slowly across the loft and swung the old doors open. One had lost the top hinge and dangled loosely, swaying slightly in the breeze. The other squeaked with rust. But the light flooded in. It took Nancy just a few seconds to figure out what had happened.

"It was no accident," she told Ned.

"How do you know?"

"Look at the rest of the bales. They're stacked far enough from the edge so they couldn't have just fallen."

"Couldn't the two that fell have been on the edge?" asked Ned.

"I don't think so," Nancy said, pointing down. "Look at the floor of the loft. It's covered with some hay, but mostly dirt. See? There's a smooth, wide track in the dirt, from the back of the loft to the edge." Nancy paused. Then she said, "It was no accident, Ned. Someone pushed those two bales from the pile at the back to the edge and shoved them over."

Nancy moved to the back of the loft and looked out of the open doors. "And here's how that someone got in and out of the loft," she said, pointing to a metal extension ladder that was propped up against the barn, right under the loft doors.

Nancy and Ned looked around a bit more, then they climbed down from the loft. Nancy returned to the stall she'd wanted to check before the bales had fallen. Sure enough, behind the stall was a kind of crawl space. She felt her skin tingling with excitement. Was this where Warren Tyler had found the Beaulieu paintings?

Ned handed the flashlight to Nancy. Turning it on, she crawled into the opening. She was inside only a short time before she came back out, a look of disappointment on her face.

"Empty," she said. "Nothing but cobwebs and hay. I guess I expected more."

"More what?" Ned asked. "If that's where the

paintings were found, why wouldn't it have been cleaned out?"

Nancy shrugged. "You never know what might have been left behind. Anyway, something just doesn't seem right."

"Maybe this isn't the place where the paintings were discovered."

Nancy shook her head. "Oh, well. I guess we might as well go home."

"I think you're right," Ned said.

As they headed back to Brian's house, Ned wondered if they should have looked around some more, maybe in some of the other buildings.

"I thought about it," Nancy said. "But whoever pushed those bales down could still have been out there."

"Do you think it was Tyler?" Ned asked.

"It could have been," Nancy admitted. "But the place has been deserted a long time. Suppose there was a family of squatters living there. Maybe they just didn't want strangers looking around."

"Well, they picked a pretty dramatic way to make their point. But I don't think you really believe that a family of squatters was responsible for letting loose those bales."

Nancy remembered the tumbling bales of hay again. She managed a slight smile. "I have a feeling we haven't seen the last of that place," was all she said.

"Do you think we should tell the police what happened?"

Nancy shook her head. "Not yet. I don't want

Lieutenant Duford to think I come running every time something happens. Let's wait."

Back at Brian's, Nancy and Ned told the others about their adventure in the barn.

"Some Mardi Gras you're having," George remarked.

"It's typical Nancy Drew," Bess joked. "Should we expect anything different?"

"I guess not," George answered. "And that's why you shouldn't feel bad about this, Brian. Nancy always manages to find a case to solve."

"I'll tell you one thing," Nancy said. "When I saw those two bales of hay coming down, I had a fleeting thought that this was my last case. And if it wasn't for Ned, it might have been."

"I'm glad he was there," Brian said. "I don't know if I could have reacted so quickly."

"Sure you would have," Ned replied.

Bess grew serious. "Listen," she said. "If someone tried to knock you out, they're not fooling around anymore."

"Right," George agreed. "Someone doesn't want you nosing around out there, or maybe anywhere else."

"I know," Nancy said. "But that leads me to believe that at least one of the people we suspect actually *is* involved in this. If The Bat were an outsider he wouldn't be too concerned with me."

"Could The Bat be someone I know?" Brian asked.

"I really can't say yet," Nancy answered. "But I hope not. Listen, I feel kind of grimy. I think I'll go upstairs and get cleaned up. Then we can grab something to eat and maybe have a little fun tonight."

"Now, that sounds like a good idea," Bess said. "You could use a break."

Nancy went upstairs. Brian headed for the kitchen. "I'm cooking tonight," he announced. "I'm making a Brian Seaton gumbo special. I'll show you how we natives eat. And Ned will be my assistant. You girls can watch."

"That's all right by us," Bess said.

The boys hustled out to the kitchen, with Bess and George following behind. Suddenly they all heard a shriek from upstairs.

The four of them raced from the kitchen and charged toward Nancy's room just in time to hear her shriek again.

Ned threw open the door to her room. Nancy was standing in the corner, her arms raised protectively in front of her face. Ned started to run in, then stepped back. Flapping wildly around the room was a large brown bat! Bess screamed. Only Brian knew what to do. He raced to the bathroom, grabbed a large towel, then rushed past Ned. Within seconds he had covered the creature in the towel. He went to the window and released it.

"Nothing to worry about," he said coolly. "They won't really hurt you."

"How'd that thing get in here?" Nancy said with a gasp.

Brian shrugged. "Who knows? If the window was open it could have come in last night and just lay low until now."

"The window *was* open," Nancy said. "But I

73

don't remember opening it. I felt the breeze as soon as I walked into the room though."

"Maybe the housekeeper opened it," Bess suggested.

"Could be," Brian admitted.

"Proves one thing, anyway," Ned remarked. "Brian acted just as fast as I did at the barn. I didn't know what to do with that thing."

"Well, I'm a bat specialist," Brian said with a grin.

"It seems like wherever we turn down here, we're running into bats, bat costumes, or bat thieves," George joked.

"That's for sure," Nancy said.

"I would have fainted," Bess said, shivering.

Nancy finished freshening up, after assuring her friends that she was okay. Brian, Ned, Bess, and George returned to the kitchen. Brian and Ned prepared the gumbo, then kept it warm until Nancy came downstairs. The food was good and the meal relaxing. While they ate, they listened to a soft-rock station on the radio.

During dinner, Nancy and her friends discussed their evening activities. Brian said he had some friends who were throwing a party, but Nancy, Bess, and George wanted to go downtown.

The decision was a compromise. They would head downtown for the festivities first, then catch the party for a few hours afterward.

They were finishing up their meal, when the music ended and the news came on. Brian got up to turn off the radio.

"Let's listen to the news," suggested Bess. "I'd

like to hear the weather report for tomorrow. I hope it's going to be sunny!"

The newscaster droned on with news from around the world. Then he said, "And in local news tonight—a theft from the Koch Gallery. A painting by Lucien Beaulieu has been stolen!"

9

A Shocking Discovery

Nancy and her friends listened for more news about the stolen painting, but that was the end of the report. Brian snapped off the radio.

"Brian, where is your father tonight? Is he in the house?" Nancy asked urgently.

"I don't really know where he is. Why?" Brian paused. "You don't think Dad will be suspected of stealing this painting, too, do you?"

"I hope not, but I've got a hunch Lieutenant Duford is going to show up here pretty soon."

Nancy was right. The lieutenant arrived within half an hour and immediately asked if Bartholomew Seaton was at home. When Brian said he didn't know where his father was, Lieutenant Duford said he would wait.

"We heard about the theft on the radio," Nancy told him. "Exactly what happened?"

"Well, as you probably know, it took place at the Koch Gallery," Lieutenant Duford said. "One of the other Beaulieus was taken."

"A street scene," Nancy murmured.

"Right."

76

"What makes you think Mr. Seaton is the thief?"

"The thief left a calling card."

"Calling card?" Nancy was puzzled.

"A live bat."

"A what!" Bess cried.

"A live bat. When we got to the gallery, a bat was just flying around in the section the painting was taken from."

"Nancy, tell Lieutenant Duford what happened to you," George suggested.

"No, no," Brian said, quickly. "That was just a coincidence."

"What happened to Nancy?" asked Lieutenant Duford curiously.

"She went to her room a few hours ago and found a live bat flying around," Bess said. "It nearly scared her to death."

"Where's the bat now?" asked the lieutenant.

"Brian caught it and let it go," Ned told him.

"The bats don't usually get in the house," Brian added. "But it does happen occasionally. I mean, this place isn't called Bat Hollow for nothing."

"Do you think the incidents are related?" Lieutenant Duford asked Nancy.

Nancy took a deep breath. "I doubt it," she said finally. "At least not to *this* theft."

Brian gave her a funny look, and Nancy hoped he didn't think she was beginning to suspect his father after all.

At that moment the front door opened. Bartholomew Seaton entered the house. He was dressed in an outfit that Nancy found somewhat out of character for him. Instead of his usual business suit, he was wearing jeans, a dark blue pullover, and a pair of black running shoes. It was the kind of outfit someone might wear if he wanted to move quickly—and remain unseen at night.

"Well, this is a happy little group," he said. "And I see that the New Orleans P.D. is here once again. What did I do this time?"

"Could you tell me where you've been the last couple of hours?" Lieutenant Duford asked rather harshly.

Mr. Seaton smiled and shook his head. "Sorry. I know it's going to make me sound like a CIA agent or something, but I can't tell you."

"I think you'd better," Lieutenant Duford told him.

"Look, how many times do I have to tell you I had nothing to do with the theft of Warren's painting?"

"That's not why I'm asking. There was a theft at the Koch Gallery tonight. Another of the new Beaulieus was taken."

"And Ferdinand accused me. Am I supposed to be surprised?"

"No one has accused you," Lieutenant Duford said sternly. "But a live bat was found in the gallery. The thief's calling card, we think. Seems like we're running into a lot of bats lately. Sound funny to you, Mr. Seaton?"

"Very funny. I guess it's just my tough luck to live in Bat Hollow and to have chosen a bat costume for the ball. Bingo! Instant suspect."

"Just tell me where you were tonight and that will end it," the lieutenant said.

"I've been looking into the possibility of raising the ransom money for *Danielle's Dream*. The people I'm involved with wouldn't want their names made public."

"Why not?" asked Lieutenant Duford.

"That's their business," Mr. Seaton replied shortly.

"I see. And do you always go to business meetings dressed like that?"

"I don't see what my choice of clothes has to do with it."

"Just looking at every angle," replied Lieutenant Duford.

"I imagine there are times when you get tired of wearing that suit of yours. I just wanted to relax, and the place I went to didn't call for a suit and tie."

Nancy could see that the lieutenant was annoyed by Mr. Seaton's answers. She had a feeling he wanted to take him to the police station again but knew that he didn't have enough evidence to go on.

"Just doing my job, sir," Lieutenant Duford said patiently. "Think about it. If you want to talk, I'm available anytime. Good night, everyone."

After Lieutenant Duford left, Bartholomew Seaton turned to Nancy.

"You know, I think I'm going to pay a visit to that man's superior," he said. "This is harassment as far as I'm concerned."

79

"Not really," Nancy said cautiously, hoping Mr. Seaton wouldn't get angry. "As Lieutenant Duford said, they're just checking on all the possibilities. It's too bad you don't feel free to tell them where you were when these things happened."

"I guess it is. But, believe me, I would lose a great deal of trust and confidence from my business associates if I did. Sometimes the things with which I'm involved are rather delicate."

"That may be true," Nancy replied, "but sometimes you have to look at it from the police point of view."

"I'll try," he said. "In the meantime I've got to shower and get ready to go out again."

Mr. Seaton left the room. For a moment, no one said a word. Brian was visibly upset. Finally he stood up and walked over to Nancy.

"I hate to say this, but you almost made it sound as if you think my father is the thief."

"That's not true, Brian," she answered. "It's just that any good detective has to keep an open mind. I wouldn't be doing my job otherwise."

"And I wouldn't have asked you to look into this if I thought you were going to turn against my father."

"I'm not turning against anyone," Nancy told him. "If you don't believe that now, I hope you will when this is over."

"I don't know anymore," Brian said, shaking his head. "I just don't know. I'm going to talk to my father before he leaves."

Brian left quickly, and no one said a word until they heard a door close upstairs.

"I was hoping that wouldn't happen," Nancy said with a sigh.

"It's not your fault," Ned spoke up. "He's upset, probably half wondering himself if his father is guilty."

"Do you think he is guilty?" Bess said to Nancy, almost in a whisper.

"Probably not, but the truth is I'm not one hundred percent sure. Not yet, anyway. In most cases there's a kind of logical sequence that leads to a solution. This case seems to be going off in several directions. Too many things don't fit into a pattern. Something's missing, and I haven't found it yet."

"The one big clue," Ned said.

They talked until they heard the door upstairs open and close. Mr. Seaton came down, dressed in a suit and tie, and followed by Brian. He bid his guests a quick goodbye and left.

"Nancy, I'm sorry," Brian said immediately. "I was off base before. My father showed me that. If he feels you're being fair about this, then I do, too. It's just that I've been so upset lately about everything."

"Don't worry about it," Nancy replied. "I think this case is getting to everyone."

"Well, now that we've got that settled," said George cheerfully, "what do you say that we *do* something? I'm ready to have some *fun*!"

"Let's go back to the French Quarter," said Nancy. "I didn't really get to enjoy it before. I know the rest of you have done some sightseeing, but—"

"The French Quarter is completely different at

night," Brian interrupted. "Sightseeing is one thing. At night the place comes to life. Even the food tastes better. And you can't see everything in one or two visits. So we've got to go back, anyway. I know this great place for jazz music. And another place for coffee and pastries."

"Pastries," repeated Bess. "What are we waiting for?"

"I'll drive, Brian," Ned offered as they left the house. "You've been chauffeuring us around since we got here. So tonight's your night off."

Brian tossed Ned the car keys, and everyone piled into the blue sedan. Ned followed Brian's directions—until they reached the edge of the French Quarter. There he got caught in a traffic jam and had to make a right turn instead of a left. There was a traffic jam in that street, too. Frustrated, he leaned on the horn.

Nancy, sitting in front, glanced at Ned. He had a look on his face that meant don't say a word. Cars and people were everywhere, other horns were blowing and music was blaring. It was a typical Mardi Gras night.

Nancy left Ned to the stop-and-start traffic jam and stared out at the crowds. Suddenly, something caught her eye. She looked again, then screamed, *"Stop! There she is!"*

Before anybody could react, Nancy had thrown open the car door and was pushing through the crowd. Ned tried to stop the car. He and the others called after her. But the people in the cars behind them were leaning on their horns and Nancy had already all but disappeared. Ned had no choice but to drive on and look for a place to park the car. Brian and Bess and George stayed with him.

"No point in *us* splitting up," George said practically. "We wouldn't know where the car was parked."

Nancy, meanwhile, was fighting the crowd. She had seen the mystery woman again—and had her in sight. The woman was about twenty yards in front of her, dressed in jeans and an oversized striped sweater. She had draped a shawl over her head, but Nancy had already caught a glimpse of her face. She was sure it was Danielle (or her look-alike) and this time, Nancy was determined to talk to her.

As Nancy drew closer, she was pushed and jostled by the crowd. She could feel her heart pounding with excitement. Finally, she caught up with the woman and put a hand on her shoulder.

"Please," Nancy said, "may I speak with you for a moment?"

The woman stopped and began to turn. As the left side of her face became visible, Nancy could see the beauty, the same look that had attracted her to the painting. It *was* the woman of *Danielle's Dream*. It had to be. But as the woman continued to turn, Nancy suddenly stepped back in horror. The other side of the woman's face was scarred and disfigured. It had obviously been horribly burned!

10

The Missing Link

Nancy's mouth dropped open, but she couldn't speak. She stared at the reddish brown scars. How the woman must have suffered when she got them, she thought. As Nancy stood there, dumbfounded, the woman turned and bolted into the crowd. Within seconds, she had disappeared again. Nancy wanted to run after her, to apologize if nothing else, but she couldn't move. She didn't even know how long she stood there before she heard Ned's voice.

"Nancy! Nancy! What happened?" he asked. "Who were you chasing?"

Bess, George, and Brian ran up behind Ned.

"Nancy! Thank goodness we found you!" exclaimed Bess. "What happened?"

"I saw her," Nancy said with a gasp. "The woman! The same one I saw the other night."

"Did you catch up to her?" asked George.

"Yes."

"Well, what happened?"

Nancy took a deep breath and began to feel calm. She didn't want to upset Brian with what

84

she'd seen. If the woman *was* his mother, Nancy wanted to choose a better time and place to tell him what she had looked like.

"Oh, it was nothing, really," Nancy said, with a slight smile. "I'll tell you about it later. Let's go have some fun!"

Brian steered them in the direction of a well-known jazz club. They listened to music for a while, then they went on to a little café for coffee and pastries. But they decided to skip the party Brian's friends were giving.

"Who needs to go to a party?" George said, as they headed down the crowded, brightly decorated streets toward the car. "Mardi Gras is one big party all by itself!"

The others agreed with George.

It was late when they reached Bat Hollow. Nancy and her friends stepped wearily inside the Seaton house and sprawled out in the living room. Brian brought everyone sodas.

Fortunately, nobody pressed Nancy to talk about her run-in with the mysterious woman. Instead, the conversation centered around the next day's parade.

"I don't think I'm going to be able to go to the parade with you," Nancy said. "I'm sorry. I have to ruin another outing."

"Come on, Nancy," Bess said. "First of all, we're used to your getting involved with a case, so you won't have ruined anything." She flashed a grin at Nancy. "Besides, we had some fun together tonight. What more could we ask for?"

"Bess is right," George said. "Anyway, we're going to the parade tomorrow, no matter what. If you can't make it because of the case, well, we'll take pictures for you."

"That would be great," Nancy said with a laugh. Then she excused herself and went up to bed. She decided to wait until morning to tell them what she'd seen. The case was getting to her and she needed sleep.

Nancy slept until almost ten-thirty the next morning. When she came downstairs, she found that Bartholomew Seaton had left the house early, and Ned had taken off with Brian for a while. So the girls were alone. Nancy finally told Bess and George what had happened the night before. As Nancy related the story over breakfast, the horror of the woman's face came back to her. Her friends felt the same horror that Nancy had experienced.

"That must have been a real shock," Bess said sympathetically. She put down her cup of tea and added, "I would have screamed."

"I almost did," Nancy admitted. "Then when I tried to say something, nothing came out. I just let her walk away."

"Don't be so hard on yourself," George said. "Think about it. You see a beautiful woman who looks exactly like the woman in *Danielle's Dream*. Then you see her again, and part of her face is horribly disfigured. As Bess said, it must have been an incredible shock."

"Which still leaves us with an unanswered question," Nancy said, buttering a slice of toast. "Who is she?"

"Just a woman who had a terrible accident,"

George replied. "The resemblance must be a coincidence."

"I'm still not sure," Nancy said. "I've got to find her again. Besides, I want to apologize to her for last night. Could I ask the two of you an awfully big favor?"

"Have we ever said no?" teased George.

"My pals," said Nancy, grinning. "Look, you're going to the parade anyway, right? Could you go down to the French Quarter a little early and just poke around some of the cafés and eating places? Ask if she's a regular anywhere, if anyone knows her name or where she lives. If they've seen her, they'll know who you're talking about right away."

"I'm not sure I'll like it," Bess said, "but I'll do it."

"Me, too," George added. "But what are you going to do while we're looking for the woman?"

"I'd like to talk to Ferdinand Koch again," replied Nancy, "or maybe Warren Tyler. I've got questions for both of them."

The girls got ready to leave. "Are you going downtown now?" George asked. "We could all go in the same cab."

Nancy shook her head. "I was hoping Ned would go with me. I'll wait a little longer. He may be back soon."

But Ned didn't return. Nancy was about to go ask Bosworth if she could borrow the jeep when the doorbell rang. Nancy answered it and found herself face-to-face with Michael Westlake.

"Ah, Ms. Drew, isn't it," he greeted her.

"Yes," said Nancy. "Hello, Mr. Westlake." She

couldn't imagine what Brian's grandfather was doing at the Seaton house, considering his relationship with Bartholomew Seaton.

"Is my son-in-law here?" asked Mr. Westlake.

"Mr. Seaton?" Nancy asked, even more surprised. She'd just decided he must have come to see Brian.

"The one and only," Mr. Westlake replied. "Unfortunately."

"No. I'm sorry, but he went out early this morning. Would you like to come in, though?" Nancy asked.

Mr. Westlake nodded and stepped inside. "Perhaps I'll wait awhile," he said. Nancy showed him into the living room.

"Mr. Westlake," Nancy said, "as long as you're here, could I—"

"Ask me a few more questions?" Mr. Westlake finished quickly. "Sure. Why not?" He glanced around the room. "Look at this room," he murmured. "Not one photo of Danielle in this entire picture gallery. The room is a shrine to my son-in-law."

Nancy cleared her throat uncomfortably. "Would you like something to drink?"

Mr. Westlake relaxed. "Thanks. I'd appreciate it," he said. He lowered himself into an armchair while Nancy went to the kitchen to pour two glasses of iced tea. When she returned, she handed one to Mr. Westlake and settled herself across from him on the end of a sofa.

Mr. Westlake sipped his iced tea thoughtfully. "Ask away," he said after a moment.

"Well," Nancy began, "I'm sure this will be

difficult for you, but I was wondering if you could tell me a little about the boating accident that killed your daughter. You said you thought Mr. Seaton was responsible."

"He certainly was," Mr. Westlake shot back. "He was a careless fool. Anyone with an ounce of sense wouldn't have put a sailboat in the water that day."

"Was the weather bad?" asked Nancy.

"No—not when he and Danielle went out. But the Coast Guard had been warning of an approaching tropical storm all morning. Even though it was a calm August day and the sky was blue, everyone *else* heeded the warnings. But not Seaton. He'd just bought a new sailboat and he was determined to go out in it."

"Wasn't he putting himself in danger, too?" asked Nancy.

"Not as much danger as he was putting Danielle in. My daughter couldn't swim."

Nancy's eyes widened.

"She didn't even like the water," Mr. Westlake continued. "In fact, she was afraid of it. But Seaton wanted to show off his new toy to her. That wasn't the worst of it, though. The worst of it was that during what he thought was a romantic luncheon at sea, my son-in-law had several drinks. Even *he* admits to that."

Nancy groaned inwardly. No wonder Mr. Westlake hated Brian's father.

"As the afternoon wore on, the storm began to brew. I'm sure Danielle pointed out the clouds to Seaton, but he was probably too happy to notice. Anyway, as you can imagine, the storm finally hit, and Seaton was in no condition to deal with it. And Danielle certainly wasn't, since she'd had so little experience with boats." Mr. Westlake paused. "You realize, of course, that what I'm telling you is really Seaton's version of the story. He's the only one who can say what happened that afternoon. There were no witnesses to the accident except Danielle, and she never got the chance to tell her story.

"Anyway, the wind was pretty fierce by then, and Seaton had been blown farther out into the Gulf of Mexico than he'd intended to sail. From what he says, the rain was pouring down so hard you could hardly see your hands in front of your face. And the wind was blowing so loudly that even when he and Danielle were shouting, they sometimes couldn't hear each other."

"Didn't they try to radio for help?" Nancy asked.

"Of course. But the storm had damaged some of their equipment. They couldn't rouse anybody. But I knew they were out there and I alerted the Coast Guard. There wasn't a whole lot they could do until after the storm let up, though."

"What finally happened?" asked Nancy.

"Well, for a while Seaton thought he could just weather the storm. But the waves grew higher and higher, and finally one capsized the boat."

"Were Mr. Seaton and your daughter wearing life preservers?"

"Of course they were," Mr. Westlake replied. "Seaton might be foolish, but he isn't crazy. He'd made Danielle put one on before the boat even

90

left the dock that morning. That's what he says, anyway. And he says he put one on himself when the storm began to brew."

"So they were both wearing them when the boat capsized," Nancy pressed. She needed to make sure of that point.

"According to Seaton," Mr. Westlake replied, nodding his head. "He was wearing his when he was rescued late that afternoon."

"How long after the beginning of the storm was that?" asked Nancy.

"About three hours," replied Westlake.

"What had happened after the boat capsized?"

"The mast and some cushions and other items were floating in the water, and Seaton and Danielle each grabbed something. Danielle hung on for as long as she could, and Seaton says he kept calling to her, trying to stay near her, but finally he called her and got no response. He couldn't see her anywhere. Her body was never found." Mr. Westlake looked away from Nancy for a moment. He pulled a handkerchief out of his pocket and dabbed his eyes.

Nancy wrote furiously in her notebook, pretending not to notice Mr. Westlake's distress. When he had recovered, Nancy looked at him. "I'm sorry," she said gently.

Mr. Westlake shrugged.

"May I ask one more question?" Nancy asked.

Brian's grandfather nodded.

"How long did Mr. Seaton hang on to the wreckage before he was rescued?"

"I'm not sure. Maybe two hours?"

Nancy nodded. But something was bothering her. How was it, she wondered, that an intoxicated man, even one wearing a life preserver, was able to stay afloat for two hours, when a sober woman wearing a life preserver wasn't able to? It didn't make sense to her, but Westlake had had enough questioning. She could see that.

Nancy changed the subject. She and Mr. Westlake talked about Brian and Emerson College and Mardi Gras. When a half hour had passed and Mr. Seaton still hadn't returned, Westlake finally decided to leave. He never told Nancy why he had come, and he didn't leave a message for Brian's father.

Ned returned shortly after Mr. Westlake left, and Nancy asked him to drive her to the Koch Gallery. With Brian headed downtown for the parade, Ned was given the jeep again.

"Who do you think has the paintings?" Ned asked as they drove along.

"I'm not sure," replied Nancy. "But I think the woman I saw fits into the case somehow. I don't know why I think that, it's just a feeling I have. And I can't get her out of my mind." Nancy told Ned what had happened the night before.

"You *really* think she's part of this?" Ned asked, frowning.

Nancy nodded. "It's just that she looks too much like the painting for it to be a coincidence."

"But, Nancy, you only saw the painting for a few minutes. How can you be so sure?"

"I'm sure. That's all I can say."

*   *   *

At the gallery, a still upset Ferdinand Koch was only too happy to talk with Nancy. He'd talk to anyone who might help him get his painting back.

"This is a terrible thing," Koch said. "There has never been a successful theft here before."

"Have there been attempts?" Nancy asked.

"Several, but our security system has stopped them even before the thieves could get inside. Then along comes this guy and he gets in and out without a whisper from security."

"How was the theft discovered?" Nancy asked Koch.

"The overnight cleaning service spotted the empty space on the wall," Koch replied.

"How would they know it was a theft?" Nancy asked. "Couldn't the painting have been removed from the exhibit for some reason?"

Koch shook his head. "No, we always tell the cleaning crew just what paintings have been removed. It's like a backup security system. If they see something out of place they notify me immediately."

"Did they notice anything else, find anything?"

"No, and the police went over the place with a fine-tooth comb. They came up empty, too. Except for the bat."

"This guy's like the wind," Ned remarked. "He comes, he goes, and it's like he's never been there."

"Except that something's missing," Nancy added.

She sat down on a chair near the door of

Ferdinand Koch's office. Ned and Koch looked at her as she went over everything in her mind once again.

"Tell me one more time how the theft was discovered, what the cleaning crew were doing, their routine, everything."

Koch sat back in his chair. "All right," he said. "Here's the routine: The cleaners come in sometime after six. First they usually dust everything —the paintings, the exhibits, the furniture. Then they empty the trash receptacles and the ashtrays in the smoking areas. They take them to be washed and disinfected. Finally they vacuum the floors. Once a week, they wash and polish them."

"But when did they notice the theft?" Nancy asked. "As soon as they came in, or later?"

"I'm not sure, but I could find out. Is it important?"

"It could be."

Koch picked up the telephone and called the head of the cleaning service. He spoke to him for a minute and then hung up.

"I think he was a little embarrassed," Koch said. "Apparently, they didn't notice the painting was gone the first time through. It was later, when they were replacing the ashtrays and trash cans."

"Near the end of their shift then," Nancy said. "That means they had already vacuumed."

"Right," said Koch, nodding.

"Could we see the bags?" asked Nancy.

"The bags?"

"The vacuum bags."

Koch looked puzzled. "Well, I guess they'd be out in the dumpster. The trash doesn't get picked up until tomorrow."

"What are you looking for?" Ned asked.

"A clue," Nancy said. "Suppose the thief got careless and dropped something? It could have been vacuumed up. It's worth a shot."

"If you don't mind, neither do I," Ned said. "Lead the way."

Koch led Nancy and Ned outside to the dumpster and pointed out the trash bags from the night before. As he did so, he wrinkled his nose and commented on the odor coming out of the huge receptacle.

"Are you sure you want to rummage through this stuff?" Koch asked Nancy.

"Absolutely sure," replied Nancy, as she and Ned began the tedious task of sifting through the vacuum bags.

"You know, some people consider garbage collections a kind of pop art," Nancy added.

"Pop art doesn't have a place in my gallery," Koch said haughtily.

"All right, Mr. Koch, we can take it from here," Nancy said. "Thanks for your cooperation."

"You're welcome. I don't see the point of all this, but do whatever you think is necessary. I'll be in my office if you need me."

"If only Bess and George could see us now," Nancy said, laughing, after Ferdinand Koch left. She and Ned were sitting on the ground behind the gallery going through one discarded vacuum bag after another. Their hands were caked with dust, grime, and lint, and much of it had spilled onto their laps.

"I think I'd rather be blitzed by three mean linebackers than do this," Ned remarked.

Nancy grinned. "I was just thinking about home," she said. "Imagine coming to the table for a piece of Hannah's double chocolate cake with hands like these."

They both laughed at that, but their laughter was interrupted when Ned suddenly said, "Ouch!"

"What's the matter?" Nancy asked.

"I just hit something sharp." Ned continued to fish around in the bag. "Here it is."

He pulled out a small object. Nancy couldn't tell what it was at first because it was so dusty. Ned took out a tissue and wiped it off.

"Hey, look at this," he said, handing the object to Nancy.

She studied it for a second. "It's a cuff link, a gold cuff link. And, look. A letter is engraved on it. An S. You just may have found something, Ned."

"S for Seaton?" Ned asked.

"I don't know," Nancy replied. "Anyone could have lost it. But it may be a clue. We'll hang on to it . . . I hope it isn't S for Seaton," she added. "Poor Brian."

Before leaving the gallery, Nancy and Ned managed to clean off most of the dust they'd acquired. Then Nancy asked Koch if anyone had reported losing a gold cuff link that day. He

96

checked his records and told them no. Nancy and Ned thanked him for his help and left.

"Let's find a pay phone," Nancy said. "I want to call police headquarters. Then I think we'll pay another visit to Warren Tyler."

Nancy and Ned were standing in front of the gallery enjoying the warmth of the afternoon sun as Ned looked around for a phone.

"There's one across the street," he said and stepped off the curb.

Nancy started to follow him. She noticed a beat-up brown station wagon sitting by the curb just twenty-five yards or so from Ned. As Nancy looked, the car suddenly leaped forward, and with a loud screech of the tires, headed straight for Ned!

11

A Call for Help

"Ned, watch out!" Nancy cried. She could see the look of surprise and then fear on Ned's face when he realized the car was coming toward him. Nancy grabbed his arm and pulled him back as hard as she could. They both tumbled to the sidewalk—and to safety.

By the time Nancy looked up, the car was squealing around the corner behind the Koch Gallery. She didn't get a chance to see the driver or catch a glimpse of the license plate.

"That was close," Ned said as he and Nancy helped each other to their feet. "Thanks for pulling one out of the way."

"We seem to be making a habit of this, don't we?" she replied.

"Unfortunately, yes," Ned said. "And this one wasn't an accident, either, was it?"

"No way. Somebody's trying to scare us off, which could mean we're getting closer."

"It also means we're being followed."

"Probably. Let's make that call to Lieutenant Duford."

Duford didn't seem concerned about the cuff link. Like Nancy, he thought it might or might not be a clue. He told her to put it in a safe place. But he was upset about the close call with the station wagon.

"Promise me you'll be careful," he said. "We don't know how dangerous this person might be. It's beginning to look as if he or she is playing for keeps."

"There's a lot at stake," Nancy agreed. "But somehow I feel this was meant to scare us, not hurt us."

"Maybe, but when someone is trying to scare you, there's always a chance you'll get hurt, too," Lieutenant Duford pointed out.

Nancy promised they would be careful. Then she and Ned drove to Warren Tyler's office to find out whether he had had any more contact with the thief.

"I'm still waiting," Tyler said. "And I can tell you it's hard on the nerves. I haven't had a good night's sleep since this happened."

Although he looked tired, Tyler was friendlier and more open than he had been previously. Since he seemed more willing to talk, Nancy decided to ask him a few quick questions.

"I'm curious," she said. "After you found the paintings, how did you discover you had something of value?"

"Everyone around New Orleans has seen some of Lucien Beaulieu's sketches and drawings. He's pretty famous locally. So I did some checking. It wasn't long before I realized they were probably worth a lot."

"And then?"

"Well, anything that sits in an old barn for ten years is not going to be in top condition. So I had the paintings cleaned up, and then I took them in to show Koch."

"You took them to the gallery?" Nancy asked.

"That's right. And Koch said they were original Beaulieus. Then he offered to buy them."

"All of them?" asked Nancy.

"Yes. And as you know, I sold him only the street scenes. I took the portrait of Danielle home with me. Everything was great—until Seaton had to mess things up."

"You still think he took it?"

Tyler nodded his head several times. "I'm sure of it. And since you're still on the case, Nancy, you can do me a favor. I'll pay you a handsome fee if you can prove Seaton is guilty and get my painting back."

"I'm not looking for a fee, Mr. Tyler," Nancy replied. "I'm just trying to get to the bottom of this."

Mr. Tyler sighed. "Are you getting close?"

"Closer. There's still some way to go."

Ned and Nancy left a few moments later. When they were outside, Nancy suggested, "Let's go to the city hall."

"City hall?" Ned repeated. "Why?"

"I'd just like to check into the backgrounds of some of the people involved in this case. It can't hurt, and considering the histories of Seaton, Tyler, and Westlake, it might help."

At the city hall, Nancy and Ned were shuttled back and forth between several departments.

Finally, they were given access to public land transaction records.

"What are you looking for?" Ned asked.

"Tyler's purchase of the Beaulieu property," she answered. "Maybe it will tell us something."

They went through the old ledgers for about twenty minutes before Nancy said, "Now, there's something that's very interesting."

"What did you find?" asked Ned.

"Guess who Warren Tyler bought that property from?" she said. "He purchased it from none other than Michael Westlake."

"Brian's grandfather! You mean *he* owned the Beaulieu property first?"

"Yes. Briefly. And he's another man who hates Bartholomew Seaton."

"But what do you think it means?"

"That's the jackpot question," Nancy replied. "So long as we're here, let's do some more digging."

Nancy and Ned spent another hour going from office to office, trying to find out more information about Warren Tyler, Michael Westlake, and Bartholomew Seaton. They found nothing they didn't already know about Westlake or Seaton. But they were surprised to learn that Tyler had suffered recent business losses and now owed a great deal of money to various people and organizations.

"What do you make of all this?" Ned asked, as they drove back toward the Seaton mansion.

"Well," replied Nancy, "the one thing Tyler and Westlake seem to have in common is their hatred for Bartholomew Seaton. The strange thing is that Tyler bought the property from Westlake at a time when he didn't seem to have much money."

"If that's the case," Ned said, "selling *Danielle's Dream* could really put Tyler back on his feet."

"Exactly," Nancy said. "Now I can understand why Tyler's been so upset by its disappearance. It also explains why he needs help in raising the ransom money."

When Nancy and Ned reached the Seaton mansion, no one was home. "Perfect," Nancy said. "I think I'll call Dad."

She made a collect call to her father's law office in River Heights. In seconds, Carson Drew had accepted the call and was on the other end.

"Hi, Dad, how are you?"

"Nancy, it's good to hear from you," Mr. Drew said. "I figured with all the fun you were having at Mardi Gras I'd be lucky to get a postcard."

"Mardi Gras has been great," Nancy said, "but I haven't had a chance to see as much of it as I'd hoped."

"You're not sick are you?" Mr. Drew asked, a sudden note of concern in his voice.

"No, no. I'm fine."

"Let me guess," Carson Drew said, suddenly understanding. "You got yourself involved with a case."

"When don't I?" Nancy said. "This one involves an art theft, and I need your connections to get some information."

"I'll try. What do you need?"

"Could you check out an art dealer named

102

Ferdinand Koch? He owns an art gallery here in New Orleans."

"Koch?"

"Yes. Just see if you can find out anything interesting or suspicious about his past. Or about the way he runs his business. Any scandals or lawsuits, especially regarding stolen art. Or forged art."

"All right, honey," Carson Drew said. "That shouldn't be too difficult. I'll see what I can find out."

"You're a lifesaver," said Nancy. "Thank you."

"I just hope you're enjoying some of Mardi Gras. Where should I call you?"

"Here at Brian Seaton's," replied Nancy. "And don't leave the information with anyone else."

"You're not involved with something dangerous, are you?" Mr. Drew asked anxiously.

Nancy paused, thinking about the falling bales of hay and the brown station wagon. "Not really, Dad. I've still had time to attend a costume ball, to eat some great Creole food, and to listen to some New Orleans jazz."

"Doesn't sound too bad. All right, I'll try to get this information for you right away. I've got a client waiting, so I'd better go."

"Okay. Give my love to Hannah."

Nancy hung up and took a deep breath. But she didn't really have time to relax. Bess and George came bursting through the front door.

"We've been trying to call you for over an hour," Bess said. "Where have you been?"

"Ned and I got tied up downtown," Nancy replied. "I thought you two were at the parade."

"We would have been, if you'd answered the phone," George said, with a trace of a smile.

"Guilty as charged. What's so important that you felt you couldn't stay for the rest of the parade?"

"We've found the mystery woman," Bess announced with a big smile.

12

An Ominous Warning

Nancy could feel her heart pounding as the girls told their story. She still wasn't sure if the mystery woman was connected with the rest of the case, but she knew she had to talk to her again.

"A number of people we talked to knew who she was," Bess said. "Once we described her face, there was no mistake."

"That was the hard part," George said. "It's not easy to describe that sort of thing to someone. I was a little embarrassed."

"I know," Nancy said, "but it had to be done. Who is she?"

"We couldn't get her last name. Her first name is Mariel," Bess said, "and she spends a lot of nights wandering around the French Quarter."

"Wandering around?" Nancy asked. "You mean like a homeless person? Does she live on the streets?"

"No, not that," George said. "She just seems to spend a lot of time down there. She shops, talks to people, just kind of hangs around."

"It's almost as if she feels more comfortable at night," Bess added. "A couple of people said she always wears a shawl or a scarf, trying to cover her face."

"I can understand that," Nancy said. "Does she have any family?"

"We're not sure," George said. "The people we talked to knew her but weren't really friends. They did say that sometimes she's with an older man."

"Her father?" Nancy asked.

"Could be," George said.

"Our best bet," Bess went on, "is to go down to the French Quarter tonight and just try to catch her at one of the places she usually visits."

"That makes sense," Nancy agreed. "Do you want to come with me?"

"We didn't come this far to quit now," George said.

"And I'm interested in seeing her myself," Bess added. "I haven't forgotten the face in the painting, either."

"I think I'll pass," Ned said. "I should spend some more time with Brian before he thinks I've forgotten about him."

"Good idea," Nancy said.

That evening, Nancy, Bess, and George were on edge as Nancy drove the jeep toward the city. They decided to park on the outskirts of the French Quarter, then walk. George said that the most likely place to find the woman was the River End Café. That was one place she always seemed to stop. Nancy asked directions, and she and her friends began their search.

As usual, the crowds were heavy, but the girls moved along without much difficulty. Finding the River End Café was another matter. The girls got lost a number of times.

After awhile, they headed toward the river and turned into a side street where there were fewer people. Instead of shops and cafés, they saw warehouses and some old apartments. They walked quickly, feeling a bit uneasy, and hoping they would find their way by the time they reached the next block. Suddenly, Nancy stopped short. She grabbed Bess and George by the arm.

"What's wrong?" Bess whispered. "Do you see her?"

"No!" Nancy replied. "Quick, duck into that alley!"

"What's going on, Nan?" George asked sharply. "What's out there?"

Nancy held a finger to her lips and peered out of the alley. Then she turned back to the girls.

"I think we're on to something. Look out there."

George and Bess peeked around Nancy.

"Isn't that Warren Tyler?" George asked.

"Yes," Nancy replied. "And the older man with him is Michael Westlake, Brian's grandfather."

The girls looked again. The two men had come out of a building and were talking with two other men at the curb. After several minutes, Tyler and Westlake got into a black limousine and drove off. The other two went back into the building.

"Hmmm," Bess said. "Do you think it has anything to do with *Danielle's Dream?*"

"One way or another," Nancy said, nodding. "I already know that Tyler and Westlake are linked." She told her friends about the sale of the property where the Beaulieu paintings had been found.

"But Tyler found the painting," George said. "And as far as we know, Bartholomew Seaton and Ferdinand Koch are the two people most interested in buying it. Where does that leave Westlake?"

"I don't know yet," Nancy replied. "Come on. Let's see what that building is."

They walked slowly past the old brick building. There was no secret about it. The building was a warehouse for Westlake Imports and Exports. With Tyler and Westlake gone, it was time to locate the River End Café.

After fifteen more minutes of searching, the three friends finally found the café. When they entered, George asked a waiter she had talked to earlier whether Mariel had been in yet that evening. He said no, and the girls slid into a booth and ordered sodas and *beignets*, a type of doughnut popular in New Orleans.

"I wonder if she'll show up," Bess said. "This is about the time she usually gets here."

"Maybe seeing Tyler and Westlake together is a turning point in the case," Nancy said. "Maybe our luck will hold and she'll show."

They sipped their drinks and ate their *beignets* and talked about Brian, his father, and *Danielle's Dream*. At one point George got restless and wondered if they should begin looking for Mariel on the streets.

"We're better off here. We could wander the streets for a month and keep missing her," Nancy replied.

"I agree with Nancy," Bess said. "Besides, it's going to take a week back in River Heights for my feet to recover from New Orleans."

The three laughed, and Nancy joked about having to return to River Heights for a "vacation" after their trip was over.

"Don't say that to Brian," George warned. "He'll never forgive himself."

"Nancy, George. Look." Bess pointed to the door. There was the woman. She was wearing faded blue jeans and a pink sweater, and draped over her shoulders and head was a pale pink shawl. She was carrying a tote bag. As the girls watched, a waiter showed her to a table. The woman set her bag on the floor and sat down, carefully keeping her face out of sight.

Nancy noticed that her scars were visible, even from across the room and in the dim light. Yet when she turned to the right, the left side of her face was beautiful. She was served a cup of coffee and a pastry, and ate and drank slowly. Nancy continued to look. No matter how much she tried to see it differently, she couldn't. The left side of the woman's face was still the perfect image of *Danielle's Dream*.

"What do you think?" Nancy whispered to Bess and George.

"That poor woman," Bess said. "I feel sorry for her."

"It *is* awful," Nancy agreed. "But take a look at the other side of her face. You saw the painting. What do you think? Am I crazy?"

Bess and George looked again, carefully, trying not to be obvious.

"I don't know," George said. "There's a strong resemblance, but really, Nancy, what kind of connection can there be?"

"The only answer I can come up with is that she's a relative. Or that it's just a coincidence," Bess said. "But she does look like Danielle."

"We've got to talk to her," Nancy said. "Come on."

The three girls made their way across the café. The woman was drinking her coffee and didn't notice them as they approached.

"Excuse me," Nancy said. "Could we talk to you for a moment? Please."

"You," the woman said, looking up. She quickly pulled the shawl over the right side of her face, as if by instinct. "Why are you following me?"

"Please," Nancy said again. "I wanted to apologize for startling you the other night. I didn't mean to do that."

The woman looked at Nancy, then at Bess and George. "What do you want from me?" she asked.

"Just a few minutes of your time," said Nancy, sitting down across from her. The table was so small that Bess and George had to sit at an adjoining table, but they were well within earshot.

"My name is Nancy Drew, and this is Bess Marvin and George Fayne. We're visiting New

110

Orleans for Mardi Gras. I believe your name is Mariel."

"How did you know that?" the woman demanded. She glanced around nervously, as if looking for an escape route.

"We learned your name when we were looking for you," Nancy said gently.

"But why are you following me?"

"The truth is that you look very much like a woman I saw in a painting. Have you ever heard of Lucien Beaulieu?" Nancy asked.

The woman didn't answer. She rose slowly from her seat.

"You'd better leave me alone," she said, quietly but firmly. "I'm warning you." She began to back toward the door and pointed a finger at Nancy. "If you don't stop following me you're— you're going to get hurt!" The woman whirled around and ran from the café.

13

Back to the Farm

"I'm going after her," George said, when the woman had disappeared into the night.

"George, are you crazy?" Bess cried. "That woman threatened us!"

"It's all right," Nancy said. "Let her go. I don't think she's a real threat. She's frightened of us, and she's just warning us away."

"Look!" Bess said suddenly. "She left so quickly she forgot her bag."

Sure enough, the tote bag was on the floor next to her chair.

"*Now* do you want me to go after her?" George asked.

Nancy thought for a minute. Then she shook her head.

"No, you'll never find her in these crowds. We'll just give the bag to the waiter and he can hold it for her—after we take a quick look."

Nancy sat down and began examining the bag. It contained a few groceries, a book, a pen, another scarf, and a pair of sunglasses. There was no wallet or identification. Suddenly Bess began to shiver. "What if this Mariel really is Brian's mother? What if she survived the accident somehow?"

"It's possible," Nancy said, "but unlikely. Now that I've seen her up close, I think she's too young."

"And what about the scars?" George asked. "How do you explain them? Danielle was in a boating accident, not a fire or something."

"A lot can happen in fifteen years," Bess pointed out.

"Well, for now," Nancy said, "let's give the waiter her bag and head back to the house."

"Fine with me," Bess said. "This has been some night. I wonder what else can happen."

"Don't ask," George joked. "I'd like nothing better than to relax and get a good night's sleep."

But when the girls walked through the front door of the Seaton mansion, they found Bartholomew Seaton and Brian having a heated argument. Ned was standing by, looking helpless.

"You're making a fool of yourself over this thing, Dad," Brian said hotly. "I've never seen you this way before."

"How dare you talk to me this way!" Mr. Seaton cried. "I thought you'd learned to show respect."

"Respect! What you're doing is going to make you the laughingstock of New Orleans. All these years you've prided yourself on your business sense. Now, because of a single painting, you're acting crazy."

Nancy, Bess, and George looked at each other, wondering what the quarrel was about.

Mr. Seaton was staring out a large picture window that overlooked the garden. Suddenly he whirled around to face Brian, his face red with anger.

"What are you complaining about?" he roared. "I've always given you everything you wanted. You've had the best of everything!"

"Maybe I'd trade it all in for a father who was just an ordinary guy. Not a man who always has to win, always has to finish first."

The elder Seaton started toward Brian. Then he stopped and looked at his son. Nancy couldn't tell if he wanted to hit him or hug him. Maybe he wanted to do both.

"You don't understand, Brian," he said, much more quietly. "My winning, or finishing first as you call it, has given us everything we have. It's given me respect in the business community."

"But if you have all the respect you say you have," Brian said, "why is everyone accusing you of taking the painting?"

"They're jealous of me, that's all," Mr. Seaton replied.

"But this is crazy. Why are you risking everything for the painting?"

Nancy's ears perked up. Risking everything?

"Brian," Mr. Seaton continued, "having *Danielle's Dream* in our home would be special. It would almost be like having your mother back."

Brian looked away. Nancy could see that he was upset. But she had to keep cool and remain a detective.

"Excuse me, Mr. Seaton," she said. "Are you

planning to get *Danielle's Dream* somehow? Does that mean that there's been more contact with the thief?"

"This is all very tricky, Nancy," Mr. Seaton said. "But I'm sure someone as smart as you are will understand. Right now, I can't say anything that might prevent the safe return of the painting."

"But are you planning to buy it?" Nancy persisted. How could he do that? The painting belonged to Warren Tyler. But if Seaton raised the ransom money, maybe Tyler would have to let him have *Danielle's Dream*.

"If things work out, there's a strong possibility that the painting will be mine," Mr. Seaton admitted.

"If things work out!" Brian exclaimed. "Why don't you tell Nancy what you told me? What's happening, Nancy, is that my father is about to be robbed!"

Brian's statement brought everyone to attention. But before Nancy could say anything, Mr. Seaton blurted out, "Robbed! That's ridiculous! I won't hear any more talk like that."

"Warren is blackmailing you, Dad! Can't you see that?"

"Call it whatever you want. It's still an opportunity I can't ignore."

"Wait a minute," Nancy said. "What is going on here?"

"It's simple, Nancy," Mr. Seaton said. "After I arrange to pay the ransom for *Danielle's Dream*, Warren has agreed to let me buy it!"

"Let me get this straight," Nancy said. "You're

going to arrange for the one-million-dollar ransom to be paid. Then, once Mr. Tyler has his painting back, you're going to buy it from him?"

"That's right."

"Right! It's all wrong," Brian shouted. "Don't you see, Dad? You're going to be paying for the painting twice. And you act as if you're getting a bargain."

"He's got a point, Mr. Seaton," Nancy said.

"I've told you my reasons," Bartholomew Seaton said. "I refuse to discuss it any further."

"Mr. Seaton," Nancy said, "I wouldn't be too hasty about this if I were you."

Seaton replied politely but firmly, "Now, please, Nancy, don't interfere where you don't belong."

"I don't have any proof yet, but there's a possibility you're being set up."

"We'll see," Mr. Seaton said, and promptly left the room.

"What did you mean by that?" Brian asked quickly. "How is he being set up?"

"I'm not one hundred percent sure yet, Brian," she said. "If I discuss this with you, you've got to promise not to do anything foolish."

"All right, I promise," Brian said.

"I have reason to believe," Nancy said, "that Warren Tyler is involved in some kind of alliance with Mr. Westlake."

"Grandfather?"

"Yes. I'm not sure of what they're planning, but I think it involves the painting. Since neither of them thinks very highly of your father, they could be trying to cheat him."

"How?"

"Let's just suppose that the theft of the painting was a setup. I don't know that it was, but let's just say so. Then, as you said, your father would be paying twice, and to the same person or persons. That's just one thing.

"Another thing that no one has thought about is the painting itself," continued Nancy. "It was stolen before the experts could take a good look at it. Suppose your father buys it and it turns out not to be a Beaulieu after all. I know he just wants to have a painting of your mother, but it would be nice if the portrait were worth something. Especially, if he's going to pay a million dollars and more to get it."

"I never thought about that," Bess said.

"But what about Mariel?" George asked.

"Who's Mariel?" asked Brian.

"That's a story in itself," replied Nancy. "She's the woman I saw that looks like your mother. She may not figure in the case, but I'm going to play out a hunch tomorrow morning. After that I may have some more answers. In the meantime, stay calm. Maybe we can still stop your father from making a big mistake."

Nancy didn't sleep well that night, and she awoke the next morning still feeling tired. But she was eager to do some detective work. After breakfast she asked Ned to drive out with her to the old farm once again.

"Haven't you had your fill of that place," George remarked as Nancy was finishing her breakfast.

"If you mean those bales of hay, yes. I wouldn't want to go through that again. But I think it's important that we check the place out once more."

Brian gave Nancy and Ned the keys to the jeep, and in no time they were at the farm. As they drove toward the buildings both of them felt nervous. The falling hay bales had seen to that. They could be in danger. Nancy wondered if they should have told the police what they were up to.

The place looked exactly as it had the first time, weathered and windblown. There were no outward signs of anyone having been there since their last visit. Still, both Nancy and Ned had an uneasy feeling as they parked the jeep and began walking toward the old farmhouse.

"What do you expect to find?" Ned asked as he looked around. "More old paintings?"

"Nothing like that," Nancy replied. "But whoever tried to scare us away the last time must be hiding something here." Suddenly she stopped and pointed to the ground. "Look, aren't those fresh tire tracks?"

"They could be. It's hard to tell."

The house was in just as bad shape as the barn. It looked like something out of a horror movie, with old wood shutters swinging in the breeze and occasionally banging against the siding. As Nancy walked across the front porch the ancient boards creaked with every step. She knocked at the door.

"Do you really expect to find someone home here?" Ned asked.

118

"Just trying to be polite," Nancy said with a grin, knocking again.

"You can tell them you're selling magazines," Ned joked.

The humor relaxed them, but as they expected, no one answered the door. Nancy tried the knob. The door was locked.

"Why would the front door of *this* place be locked?" she wondered. "There are twenty easy ways to break in here."

"Beats me," Ned said.

"Well, I'll use one of the twenty."

Ned rolled his eyes. "You've got to be kidding. Now it's breaking and entering. What next?"

"First things first," Nancy replied. "Come on."

Nancy and Ned walked along the porch. Ned tried the first window he came to and it opened. He calmly stepped over the sill and smiled at Nancy. She nodded and followed him. They were inside the house.

"See, I told you it would be easy," Nancy said. "You're a natural detective."

"Okay, let's investigate."

They explored the house slowly and carefully, awed by the silence. The entrance hall and living room were both full of dust and cobwebs. Junk and debris was everywhere. There was no real furniture in sight, only some broken pieces from the past.

"I don't think anyone's here," Ned said in a low voice.

"No," Nancy said, adding, "Mr. Tyler has a long way to go if he plans to fix this place up."

119

"I . . . Hey, Nancy, look at this."

Ned had stopped to look inside a large closet. He was pulling out a canvas tarpaulin covered with a colorful splattering of paints.

"I wonder what that's from," Nancy said. "It's covered with paint, but do you see anything around here that's been painted? And these are oils, I think, the kind an artist uses, not the kind you paint a house or furniture with."

"Maybe it belonged to Lucien Beaulieu," offered Ned.

"No way. This stuff is fresh. Someone was working here, painting."

Nancy stooped down and rummaged behind the cloth. Her hand touched cobwebs. Then she gasped and jerked her hand back in surprise.

"What is it?" asked Ned.

"I found a secret compartment or something. I felt part of the wall slide back. Did you bring the flashlight from the jeep?"

Ned shook his head.

Nancy reached her hand back into the compartment. Her fingers closed over an object. She brought it out into the light and stood up to examine it. "I never expected to find something like *this*."

"What is it?" asked Ned.

"It's a diary from the year Brian's mother died. And the name inside the cover is Danielle Seaton."

14

Danielle's Secret

"What on earth is a diary belonging to Brian's mother doing out here?" asked Ned incredulously.

"I don't know," replied Nancy. "Mrs. Seaton did take painting lessons from Beaulieu, and she must have posed for the portrait Tyler found, but—well, I have a feeling the answer to your question is right here. Let's open the diary and take a look."

"Let's find someplace to sit down first, though," said Ned.

Nancy and Ned walked through the first story of the late artist's home. They discovered that the kitchen had the most light, so they settled themselves on the floor, leaning back against some rickety cabinets.

Nancy lifted the cover of the diary. "Boy, is this creepy," she said.

"I know. Brian's mother. It's like she's come to life," replied Ned.

"It's not that so much. It's . . . you know, reading someone's personal, private thoughts.

121

Thoughts that weren't meant to be read by anyone except the writer."

"I know what you mean," Ned replied, nodding.

"Okay," Nancy said. "Here goes." She opened to the first page.

It was blank.

So were the next page and the next. She and Ned glanced at each other.

Nancy flipped ahead. "Here," she said. "The entries begin on April twenty-fifth. I wonder why."

"Read," commanded Ned.

"'The news isn't good,'" Nancy read slowly. "'Lucien is wonderful. He lets me come to his farm and paint or just sit in the garden and think. He knows I need an escape.'"

"From Seaton?" Ned interrupted.

"I don't know. 'Tomorrow more tests with Dr. Withers,'" Nancy read. "That's the end of the entry." She turned the page.

"Tests with Dr. Withers," Ned repeated. "A professor? Was she taking courses?"

Nancy read the next entry. "'April twenty-sixth. Dr. Withers said I won't know the results for a week. How odd that I pour out everything to Lucien but haven't been able to bear telling Bartholomew. I know he loves me very much, but he can't stand weakness of any kind.'"

Nancy moved on to the next page. "'I know I'm not much of an artist,'" she read, "'but Lucien is so encouraging. He reminds me of my grandfather. I am lucky to have this sanctuary.'"

"It doesn't say anything about Beaulieu painting her," Ned said, sounding frustrated. "Skip ahead. Let's find out about those test results."

Nancy turned several pages and began skimming the entries. After a moment, she let out a low whistle.

"What is it?" asked Ned.

"Ned, this is so awful. The test results. Withers was a medical doctor. Brian's mother had a brain tumor."

Ned grabbed the diary from Nancy. "Where does it say that?"

Nancy pointed to the entry. "No two ways about it."

"You're not kidding," Ned said. " 'Six months to a year to live,' she writes."

"Ned, Michael Westlake told me that the boating accident happened in August," Nancy said suddenly.

"That's right," Ned said. "I know because Brian once told me he always hated August. When I asked him why, he said it was the month his mother died in."

"August," repeated Nancy slowly. "Four months after Mrs. Seaton found out she had cancer. That's very interesting."

"Why?"

"Think about it. What if Mrs. Seaton let herself die during the accident? Maybe she saw it as an easy way out. She could avoid all the pain and the hospitals and chemotherapy. She probably spared Brian all those months of seeing his mother as a very sick woman. He never had to remember her that way. I wish her body had been found after the accident, though."

Ned stared at Nancy in disbelief. "You're not thinking that maybe—somehow—she's alive after all? That Mariel is really Mrs. Seaton? How could that be?"

"No, no. That's not what I mean. I'm sure Brian's mother is dead. I'd just be interested to know if she died with her life preserver on. If she didn't, it would only be because she took it off. Which would be as near as we'll ever come to proof that Mrs. Seaton wanted to die."

"I guess we'll never know," said Ned.

"I guess not. But let's read the rest of the diary. Look, it only goes to August second."

Ned and Nancy read Mrs. Seaton's description of the last few months of her life. Slowly her story unfolded. She had begun taking painting lessons from Beaulieu as an escape from Brian's father, whom she both loved and felt intimidated by. The marriage hadn't been unhappy, but it hadn't been entirely happy, either. In Beaulieu, Danielle had found a kindly and sympathetic old man, a patient listener, someone she could trust with her secrets. She told him about her illness— she told no one else. She didn't want to upset her husband, her young son, or her father.

Danielle and the artist became great friends. Beaulieu understood about the diary Danielle felt compelled to keep once she realized she was sick. When Danielle told him that she wanted the artist to hide the diary for her, he had obliged. He had taken Danielle's secret to his grave.

"This is so odd," Nancy mused when she had finished reading. "There's no mention at all of

Danielle posing for the portrait. Don't you think that's strange, Ned?" she asked.

"Very strange," agreed Ned. Then he added, "What should we do with the diary?"

"I have to think about that," Nancy replied. "It does shed a different light on Bartholomew Seaton, the prime suspect. But it doesn't prove a thing—only that Mr. Seaton isn't the ogre Westlake and Tyler and probably half of New Orleans think he is. It doesn't give us any clues about the theft. And Danielle obviously wanted her secrets kept secret."

"But that was fifteen years ago!" protested Ned. "Don't you think the truth should come out? I think Brian should know. His feelings for his father are very mixed. He should know what happened to his mother."

"I agree . . . I think," Nancy said. "What I'm going to do is take the diary with me. We can decide what to do with it later."

"*Can* you take it?" Ned asked. "It belongs to Warren Tyler now."

"No," Nancy said quietly. "it belongs to Lucien Beaulieu, and I have a feeling he would want Brian and his father to have it . . . sometime."

Nancy and Ned left the farmhouse then. Nancy decided to drive and she took the wheel of the jeep as they began the trip back to Bat Hollow.

As the jeep bounced along the dirt road that led back to the highway, Nancy noticed that a car fell in about a hundred yards behind them. It began to gain on them rapidly.

"Looks like we've got a cowboy on the road," Ned remarked, turning around to look. "There's a guy in it. Slow down and let him pass."

"Uh-oh," Nancy said. "I hate to say this, but that's not just some cowboy. The car is the brown station wagon, the one that tried to run you down."

Nancy took her foot off the gas. The station wagon was gaining fast, and as she looked in the rearview mirror, it didn't seem to be pulling out to pass. Nancy felt butterflies in her stomach, and she gripped the steering wheel harder. She looked in the mirror again. The car was almost on top of them.

"Step on it, Nancy, he's going to—"

Ned stopped speaking abruptly as the station wagon slammed into the back of the jeep, jarring it hard. Nancy had to struggle to make sure she didn't lose control of the vehicle. She stepped on the gas. The jeep shot forward, but the station wagon accelerated and kept pace.

"I don't know if I can outrun him," Nancy said. "I think he wants us off the road."

The station wagon slammed into the back bumper of the jeep a second time. Again, Nancy was able to control the vehicle, but she didn't know how many more shocks like that she could take. She also remembered they were about to reach a sharp curve with a deep gully on the right side of the road. That's where the station wagon would most likely make its move.

"Nan," Ned said, trying to stay calm, "remember that defensive driving course you took last year?"

She nodded, still concentrating on the road and the car behind them.

"Use that stop and spin maneuver you told me about."

Nancy nodded again. "I plan to," she said. "Up there. I'm going to do it on the curve."

Nancy gritted her teeth. The curve was ahead, and so was the steep gully with only a low guard rail for protection. It wouldn't take much for a vehicle to hurdle the rail and plunge into the gully. Nancy knew what she had to do. Only this time it wasn't just a driving test. It was the real thing, and their lives might be on the line.

As she started to swing into the curve, the station wagon moved to the outside. Sure enough, the driver was going to try and force her off the road into the gully. She was on the curve when the other car pulled even with her. To her right was the gully. The station wagon slammed into the jeep, causing it to swerve dangerously to the right.

The gully beckoned.

"Ned!" Nancy screamed. "I'm not sure I can pull it back. We may be going over. Hang on!"

15

The Circle Closes

Nancy turned the wheel to the left as hard as she could and got the jeep back on the road. But the station wagon was zeroing in for another hit.

"Do it now!" yelled Ned.

As soon as she saw the station wagon make its move, Nancy hit the brakes. Her timing was perfect. The station wagon hurtled past them. Without the jeep there to bump, it went out of control. Nancy then spun the wheel to the left again and skidded around in an almost perfect circle. She brought the jeep to a stop in the middle of the road.

The station wagon, in the meantime, slid along the guard rail and came to a halt in a deep shoulder. The driver tried to get the car out, but the wheels just spun in the soft sand, digging deeper. It was stuck.

"Beautiful driving, Nancy," Ned said breathlessly. "You okay?"

She nodded.

"Then let's get out of here," he said.

"Right. But first, let's get his license number,"

128

said Nancy. She threw the jeep into gear and sped past the still-stuck car.

"Guess what," Ned said. "No plates. That guy's smart."

"He probably has them in the front seat, and he'll put them on as soon as we're out of sight."

Down the road Nancy wiped her forehead. "Boy, that was close," she said. "I don't want to have to do that again."

"You were great," Ned said. "Lucky thing I wasn't driving. I couldn't have done that."

"We practiced it enough when I took the course, but when you have to do it under pressure, it's a whole different ballgame."

"Who *was* the guy?" Ned asked, almost as an afterthought.

"Probably the same one who tried that little number with the bales of hay," Nancy said. "And, of course, he was the guy who tried to run you down in front of the gallery. I'm wondering if Tyler and Westlake are involved."

"You think they'd go that far?"

"Look at it from their side," Nancy said. "There's a whole lot at stake, one million dollars for starters. I still think they're just trying to scare us off."

"If it weren't for you, that goon could have done a lot more than scare us. Do we go to the police now?"

"Not just yet. That guy will be long gone by the time the police get here. For now, we sit tight."

Nancy and Ned stopped at a roadside diner for a quick lunch. When they got back to the Seaton mansion, they found Bess, George, and Brian finishing their lunch. Nancy told them about the close call with the station wagon—they could hardly believe it.

"You could have been killed!" Brian exclaimed. "What have I gotten you into?"

"Hey, this is normal for Nancy," Bess said. "She's been in tougher scrapes than this."

"And because of her, so have we," George added, with a laugh.

"I don't know how you can joke about it," Brian said. "This is serious business."

"You're right," Nancy said. "It *is* serious business. And we can't waste any time."

"By the way, Nancy, your father called," George said. "But Bosworth answered the phone and your father didn't leave any message."

"I'd better call him back right away."

Carson Drew's secretary said he was still out to lunch. She would have him return Nancy's call as soon as he got in. Nancy then asked Brian where his father was.

"He went out very early this morning and said he didn't know when he would be back."

"Did he seem nervous or anxious?" Nancy wanted to know.

"Well, he skipped breakfast. Usually the only time he does that is when there's some big business deal going on."

"That's what I was afraid of," Nancy said. "Sometime soon a great deal of money is going to change hands."

"What can we do?" Ned asked.

"First, I want to get in touch with my father."

"Why don't we wait out by the swimming

pool?" Brian suggested. "We can bring the cordless phone with us so we don't miss the call."

"Great idea!" Bess exclaimed. "I haven't gotten nearly enough use of my bathing suit down here. Besides, I want to work on my tan."

"I like Brian's idea, too," Nancy said with a smile. "Let's go!"

Ten minutes later, Nancy, Bess, George, Ned, and Brian had changed into their swimsuits and were sitting by the pool. Brian placed the cordless phone on a table next to Nancy.

Bess stretched herself out on a lounge chair. "Will somebody grease me up, please?" she asked lazily.

George rolled her eyes. "You are a lazy lump, Bess Marvin."

"At least oil my back for me. I don't want to tan unevenly."

"Oh, no, we couldn't have that tragedy," said George, but she did rub lotion on Bess's back before diving gracefully into the pool.

Brian followed George, and Ned followed Brian. The three of them swam laps and were trying to convince Bess and Nancy to take part in a mini-Olympics, when the phone finally rang. Nancy reached for it quickly. "Hi, Dad," she said. She listened for several moments, then smiled and thanked her father for his help.

"Very interesting," she announced as soon as she'd gotten off the phone.

Ned, George, and Brian had climbed out of the pool and were waiting, dripping wet, for news.

"I asked my father to check up on Ferdinand Koch, and guess what he found out," said Nancy.

131

"What?" chorused the others.

"Koch has a police record a mile long—but his last arrest took place over twenty-five years ago. Since then, he's been clean. His gallery is highly regarded, and he's done a lot of nice things with his money—opened a library, started art scholarships, you know."

"What was he arrested for?" asked Brian.

"Well, that's the really interesting part. All of his arrests were for shoplifting, property damage, and petty theft—except for one. When he was nineteen, he was arrested for being involved with . . . an art forgery scam."

16

The Final Clue

"Wow," Bess said slowly. "Art forgery . . ." Her voice trailed off.

George, Ned, and Brian had toweled themselves dry while Nancy was telling them about her phone conversation. They sat in a row on one of the lounge chairs and looked at Nancy solemnly.

"Koch has been saying he thinks the Beaulieu street scenes might be forgeries," Nancy said. "Now we find out that Koch was once involved in an art forgery scam." She frowned.

"What are you saying?" asked Ned.

"I'm not sure. For a while I thought maybe *Koch* had stolen *Danielle's Dream* so he could have a chance to examine it before he made Tyler another offer for it. Then I thought maybe the business about the three street scenes being faked was a smoke screen—you know, to distract us from the theft. But what would they have to do with—?" Nancy paused. "Brian, could I borrow the jeep? I think I'd better have another talk with

133

Koch. I've got a few questions for him about those paintings."

"Want me to come with you?" asked Ned.

"No, thanks," Nancy said. "I'll go by myself. Maybe I'll take a look around the French Quarter afterward. I haven't seen much of it—at least not during the day—and I haven't even bought any souvenirs. I'd better get something for Dad and Hannah."

Nancy stood up and headed into the house. George and Bess followed her. "Are you *sure* you don't want someone to come with you?" asked Bess.

"I'm sure," Nancy said. "You and George have done enough detective work this vacation. You stay here with Ned and Brian and have fun. I'll only be gone a couple of hours."

"Well, if you're sure—" Bess began.

"Positive," Nancy replied before Bess could finish. She grinned. "Go work on your tan. Otherwise, when we get back to River Heights, no one will believe you've been away. And you go swim, George. Challenge Ned to a race. I bet it will be a close one."

Bess and George returned to the pool, and Nancy changed her clothes quickly. Then she grabbed her purse, found the keys to the jeep, and jumped into the car. She hoped she could find her way to the Koch Gallery without too much trouble. Nancy turned on the radio and pulled out of the Seatons' front drive.

It was almost five o'clock when Nancy reached the gallery. She had some difficulty finding a parking spot, and by the time she had dashed up the steps, a guard at the front door was turning people away.

"Sorry," he said to Nancy, as she tried to brush by him. "No more visitors after five. The gallery's closing."

"Oh, but I'm not here to see the gallery," Nancy said. "I'm here to see Ferdinand Koch. I . . ."

"Just a moment," said the guard. He turned and spoke to a young woman behind him. The woman hurried off. When she returned a moment later, she looked puzzled and told Nancy, "It seems that Mr. Koch has forgotten about your appointment. He's already left for the day."

"Oh," replied Nancy, in a disappointed voice.

"Who shall I say was here?"

"Um, Ms. . . . Ms. Jones," said Nancy, and rushed off. I can't believe I just said that, she thought. And I can't believe I wasted this trip. I should have called first.

Nancy climbed into the jeep and headed for the French Quarter. At least she could buy her souvenirs. She managed to find a parking spot, locked the car, and joined the crowds of people on the streets. In a dark, dusty bookstore she bought an old volume called *A History of New Orleans* for her father. She found Hannah's present in a candy store—a big bag of homemade pecan pralines and the recipes for making various desserts with them. She hoped Hannah would use the recipes as much as she'd enjoy the candy.

Nancy left the candy store and turned down a narrow street. She passed a fortuneteller, a tarot card reader, and a palm reader. Then she turned a corner—and found herself in front of the River End Café. She smiled. When we want to find this place it takes hours, she thought. Now I practically stumble over it.

Nancy sat down at a small table in the back of the café. She ordered coffee and a *beignet*. While she waited to be served she sampled the pralines she'd bought Hannah. When her food arrived, she pulled *A History of New Orleans* out of her shopping bag and thumbed through it. She wasn't sure how long she had been lost in the book when she glanced up and saw a woman leaving the café.

It was Mariel!

Nancy didn't waste a second. She slapped some money on the table, gathered up her bags, and rushed out of the café. According to George and Bess this was not Mariel's usual time to stop at the café. Nancy couldn't believe her luck. And she was not going to let Mariel get away. Talking to her had been no help, and Nancy was sure she was hiding something.

Mariel was walking down the street the café stood on, heading east. She didn't seem to be in a hurry. Once she stopped in a store, and several times she waved to people she passed. The sky grew darker as evening fell, but Nancy had no trouble following Mariel. And Nancy was grateful for the dusk because she didn't have to worry that Mariel might spot her.

Mariel walked and walked. Nancy followed her for what seemed like miles. She followed her out of the French Quarter, through the city, and finally to a neighborhood with small houses and matchbox-size yards. Mariel turned into the driveway of a white house with a sagging porch and crooked shutters.

Nancy caught sight of the car in the driveway, and gasped. It was a station wagon—a beat-up brown station wagon. She was sure it was the same car that had nearly run Ned down and had tried to run the jeep over the side of the road. So Mariel *was* tied to the theft somehow, whether she admitted it or not. And maybe Westlake and Tyler were innocent after all. Had Mariel been the driver of the station wagon? Nancy and Ned had thought it was a man behind the wheel, but maybe they'd been wrong.

The back license plate of the station wagon had been replaced. Nancy jotted down the number. Then she waited across the street until Mariel was safely in the house. When Nancy could see her in one of the first-floor rooms, she began to cross the street. She was halfway to the house when Mariel suddenly walked over to the window, opened it, and peered out. Nancy looked around in a panic. She ducked behind a parked car and crouched down, hoping she hadn't been seen. She let five minutes go by. Then she stood up slowly. No one was at the window.

Nancy crept up to the house and flattened herself against the wall, next to the open window.

I wish I could see inside, she thought. But while she was deciding if it was safe simply to look in, she heard voices.

"Dad, you work too hard," said one voice. Nancy was sure it belonged to Mariel. "You don't have to do all this for me."

"I know I don't," said a man's voice, "but I want you to have that operation. Then you'll be my beautiful Mariel Devereaux again."

So *that* was Mariel's last name, Nancy thought. Devereaux!

"But it would be years before we saved enough money," Nancy heard Mariel say.

"No, it won't," replied the man shortly. "I've been working on a plan, I'll get the money."

"What kind of plan?" asked Mariel suspiciously.

"Just a plan," said her father. "Now leave me alone."

Silence. Nancy checked her watch. She would wait for three minutes of silence before she did anything. Nancy crouched in the stubbly grass, hoping fervently that neither Mariel nor her father would come to the window.

Night had fallen and the neighborhood was very dark. Most of the streetlights were out. Nearby, a twig snapped. Nancy jumped. An orange tabby cat emerged from under a bush, meowed loudly, and trotted over to Nancy. Nancy petted it, hoping it would go away quietly. It did.

I should have phoned the Seatons, Nancy thought a moment later. Ned and Bess and George are probably frantic by now.

At last Nancy dared to turn around. She rose up until her eyes just peeked over the edge of the sill.

The room inside was brightly lit, but sparsely furnished. In the middle of the room stood an artist at an easel. His back was to Nancy, but almost immediately he turned around completely, and Nancy looked him full in the face. Just when Nancy was about to duck, he turned around again. Apparently, he hadn't noticed her.

Nancy could see only part of the painting he was working on, but she noticed that it looked a lot like the street scenes she had seen in the Koch Gallery. What was more interesting, however, was the stand that was next to the easel. Propped open on it was a fat book. Nancy could just make out the big print across the top of the left-hand page. It read Lucien Beaulieu: His Work. On the facing page was what Nancy knew to be a "typical" Beaulieu street scene. And the upper right corner of the painting in the book was identical to the corner of the painting that Nancy could see on the easel.

Nancy's jaw dropped open.

Mariel Devereaux's father was copying an original Beaulieu painting.

17

The Chase Is On

Nancy crept quietly away from the house. The pieces of the puzzle were falling into place. The Devereauxs were definitely involved with the Lucien Beaulieu mystery. It was time to find out more about them—and the person who could give her the most help with that was Lieutenant Duford.

Nancy walked several blocks and found a pay phone. She called a cab, asked the driver to take her back to the jeep, then drove to the police station, hoping fervently that Lieutenant Duford would be there. When she saw him bent busily over his desk, she sighed with relief.

"Lieutenant Duford!" she exclaimed.

"Hi, Nancy," he replied, glancing up. "How's the case coming? Have a seat."

"It's . . . intriguing. Listen to this." She explained what had happened that evening.

Lieutenant Duford raised his eyebrows.

"I know the man's last name and where he lives. And I've got his license plate number. Is that enough information for you to find out something about his background? I've got to find some link between him and Mr. Tyler or Mr. Seaton—or *something* connected with the case."

"If he's got a police record, it's plenty of information," Lieutenant Duford replied. "Let's run it through the computer."

"Interesting," Nancy was saying. An hour had gone by. She'd called Ned to tell him what she was doing and that she was safe. Now Lieutenant Duford had returned with a printout about a forty-eight-year-old artist named Max Devereaux.

"Two arrests for petty theft," said Lieutenant Duford, reading over Nancy's shoulder. "He seems to be a sort of down-and-out type. Struggled to make it as an artist but never succeeded. Wife died, daughter badly burned in an accident when she was seventeen."

"Look at *this*," Nancy said. "He was once employed as a caretaker by Michael Westlake. Twenty-two years ago. That was probably during the time Danielle Westlake was going out with Brian's father."

"So?" the lieutenant said, frowning.

"Devereaux would have known all about the rivalry between Seaton and Tyler. And he's a painter. *And* I saw him copying a Beaulieu. I'm willing to bet the ransom note was from him. I think Devereaux painted *Danielle's Dream* just so he could steal it back. Now he's counting on getting the one million dollars. He figured that with Tyler, Seaton, and Westlake interested in the portrait, he'd be bound to get the money.

Then he would have the money for his daughter's operation. And he'd be able to live the way he's always wanted to."

"It's possible," said Lieutenant Duford.

"He didn't even need to see pictures of Brian's mother. He knew what she looked like. He used his daughter as the model. She looks just like the real Danielle. The only thing is, there's no way to prove any of this—yet," Nancy went on. "This is all just a theory."

"Hey, Lieutenant! Telephone!" a uniformed officer called from across the room.

"Excuse me a second," said the lieutenant.

Nancy sat staring at the computer printout.

In a moment Lieutenant Duford returned, looking excited. "Well," he said, "we might not have proof now, but I have a feeling we will tomorrow!"

"What do you mean?" asked Nancy, jumping to her feet. "What happened?"

"Warren Tyler just received another ransom note. This one included instructions from the thief on where and when to meet him to exchange *Danielle's Dream* for the money. The police will stake out the drop, of course, and I want you to come with me, Nancy. If Devereaux is behind all this, you can identify him!"

At nine o'clock the next evening, Nancy and Lieutenant Duford were sitting in an unmarked car at the place the exchange—one million dollars for *Danielle's Dream*—was supposed to occur. The follow-up ransom note had instructed Tyler to show up at nine-thirty at Dave's Dogs, a run-down hot dog and hamburger joint at the edge of a parking lot in a seedy section of New Orleans. Tyler was to arrive alone in his own car and wait for someone to approach him. The exchange was to be made without Tyler leaving his car. Tyler was not to bring the police, but he had called Lieutenant Duford, anyway, as soon as he'd gotten the note.

Nancy and the lieutenant had been sitting at the edge of the parking lot since six that evening —just in case the thief was suspicious of the police and had been casing the area. Two more unmarked police cars were nearby, one across the street from the parking lot, another half a block away from Dave's Dogs.

Warren Tyler knew about the stakeout. He would arrive at Dave's Dogs on schedule with a suitcase containing one million dollars in unmarked bills. Michael Westlake and Mr. Seaton had both been working on raising the ransom money, and had come up with the cash. Tyler was insistent that the bills be unmarked, even though the police wanted to mark them. He was afraid of doing anything that might make Devereaux suspicious, and he was nervous enough knowing that three police cars would be nearby.

Nancy checked her watch for what seemed like the hundredth time in the last five minutes.

"Relax," Lieutenant Duford told her.

"I can't."

The minutes crawled by. At 9:25, a red sports car pulled up in front of Dave's Dogs.

"There's Tyler," said Lieutenant Duford. "I hope he remembers his instructions."

143

Warren Tyler sat stiffly in the car. Seven more minutes crept by.

"Our thief is late," the lieutenant commented.

"I hope we didn't scare him off somehow," said Nancy.

And at that moment, a brown station wagon turned the corner and parked opposite Tyler's car so that the drivers were facing each other. The front door of the station wagon opened. A man wearing a nylon stocking over his head so that his face looked distorted and expressionless stepped out. He approached Tyler's car, a large flat package under one arm. Then he motioned for Tyler to roll down his window.

Tyler's window opened, and Nancy could see him stick a suitcase through it. The stocking-masked man checked through the bills, snapped the case shut, left the package leaning against Tyler's car, and made a run for his own car. Just as he was about to get in, Nancy heard a car door slam and feet running.

"What—?" Lieutenant Duford began to say.

Two police officers had gotten out of their car and were crossing the street to the station wagon.

Lieutenant Duford slammed his fist on the steering wheel. "They're too early!" he cried. "Stay here, Nancy." He jerked the car door open and jumped out.

Nancy did as she was told. She tried to see what was going on, but the scene was confusing. The station wagon looked empty. Five police officers, including Lieutenant Duford, were converging on the scene.

Suddenly Nancy saw what the police couldn't

see: a figure heading for an alleyway. She was out of the police car in a second.

"Lieutenant Duford!" she shouted. "Over there!"

The police cornered the figure in an instant. He was led back to one of the unmarked cars where Lieutenant Duford frisked him.

Nancy crossed the parking lot slowly.

"Nancy!" The lieutenant called, waving to her.

When Nancy reached him, he pulled the stocking off the man they had caught. "Is this the person you saw last night?" he asked.

"Yes, it is," replied Nancy.

"And is that the car that tried to run Ned down?" Lieutenant Duford pointed to the brown station wagon.

"Yes, it is. It also tried to run us off the road."

Max Devereaux kicked angrily at a stone.

Warren Tyler looked at Nancy with relief and curiosity.

"Okay," said Lieutenant Duford. "Everybody down to the station. Nancy, you can call the Seatons from there. I think they'll want to join us. Devereaux, you can tell your story to everyone at once."

"I have a feeling," said Nancy, "that this is going to be one interesting night."

18

Danielle's Dream

It was an odd group of people that gathered at the police station that night. There was Max Devereaux, tense and angry. Mariel Devereaux sat next to him, looking nervous and confused. Her father had insisted that she be called immediately. Brian and his father sat stiffly next to Nancy. Only Warren Tyler looked pleased. All he cared about was the painting, and now he had it back. In the center of the group stood Lieutenant Duford.

"Would you like to tell us what happened?" the lieutenant asked Devereaux.

Max Devereaux scowled. "No."

"We've got a pretty good idea already," Lieutenant Duford informed him. "Ms. Drew figured it out. You can let all these people hear her version—or you can tell them your own."

"I did it for her," Devereaux mumbled.

"Who is 'her'?" asked Lieutenant Duford.

"For Mariel. My daughter."

Mariel's head snapped up. She stared at her father.

"I did it to pay for an operation. Mariel needs plastic surgery."

At the mention of surgery, Mariel dropped her head again. She pulled her scarf more tightly around her face.

"Do any of you know how much plastic surgery costs these days?" Devereaux said gruffly.

"I'm sure it's expensive, but it won't cost one million dollars," said Mr. Tyler.

Devereaux squirmed in his chair. "Well, no . . ."

"Why don't you start at the beginning?" asked Lieutenant Duford.

So Max Devereaux began his story. Nancy had guessed much of it correctly. When Devereaux was Michael Westlake's caretaker he'd learned about the rivalry between Tyler and Seaton. He'd also discovered how the rich live. After he left Westlake's employ he struggled to support himself as a painter. His wife had died soon after his daughter was born, and Mariel had been the one joy in his life.

Then, when Mariel was seventeen, she was badly burned in a fire. Devereaux tried to save the money necessary for the plastic surgery that could make her beautiful again, but he was never able to. Then he learned that the farm of Lucien Beaulieu, the famous local artist, had been sold, first to Westlake, then to Tyler. He remembered the boating accident that had killed Danielle Seaton, and he remembered Tyler and Seaton's love for her.

Devereaux's plan began to take shape. He studied Beaulieu's style and painted

"Danielle's" portrait, using his daughter as the model. Then, knowing that Danielle had taken lessons from Beaulieu, he made many trips to the late artist's farm, adding background to *Danielle's Dream* so the painting would look authentic. He also painted a number of farm scenes. At home he copied other works by Beaulieu. He hid *Danielle's Dream* and the street scenes in the barn, with the intent that Tyler would find them.

Devereaux planned to sell more fake Beaulieu paintings to museums and collectors. But his big scheme was to steal *Danielle's Dream* from Tyler and ransom it. He had asked for more money than he needed for the plastic surgery, but Mariel really did come first. Devereaux's love for her had prompted the crime.

When Devereaux stopped speaking, everyone had questions.

"So *Danielle's Dream* isn't really a painting of Danielle?" asked Warren Tyler. He looked crushed.

Devereaux shook his head. "No. It's my Mariel."

"And the street scenes Tyler found in the barn and sold to Ferdinand Koch are forgeries?" asked Nancy.

"Yes," admitted Devereaux.

"What do you know about the theft from the gallery?" asked Lieutenant Duford sharply.

"What theft from the gallery?" Devereaux replied.

148

"One of the street scenes was stolen."

"It wasn't me," said Devereaux. "I don't know anything about that."

"I've got a question," Brian spoke up, and everyone turned to him. He'd been quiet all evening. "Who dropped the bales of hay on my friends? You?" he pointed accusingly at Devereaux.

"Yeah. They were nosing around the farm. Made me nervous. I'd come so far with my plan . . . all that work. I didn't want a couple of kids to ruin everything."

Nancy was about to object to being called a kid, but decided against it. Instead she said, "And you tried to run Ned down."

"Ned? That his name? Yeah, I did."

"And you tried to run us off the road."

Devereaux nodded. He looked disgusted with all the questioning.

"Were you dressed as a bat the night you stole the painting from Tyler's house?" Brian asked Devereaux.

"Yup. Pretty good costume."

Bartholomew Seaton shot a triumphant look at Warren Tyler.

Nobody spoke for a few moments.

At last Lieutenant Duford said, "Well, I guess that about wraps things up for now. Devereaux, you come with me. The rest of you are free to go."

Nancy left the police station with the Seatons and Warren Tyler. She should have felt wonderful—but her last glimpse inside the room was of an anguished Mariel Devereaux clinging to her father.

"Ah. Rays, come and get me," said Bess happily. "This is your last chance to make me tan."

"We still have tomorrow morning," Nancy pointed out.

"Not really. We'll be packing then."

Nancy, Bess, George, Brian, and Ned were lazing around the pool. It was their final afternoon in New Orleans—the day after Max Devereaux had been caught. Bess, George, and Ned were still asking a million questions and were indignant that they hadn't been invited to the police station the previous night. But they *had* been around for some excitement that morning: Ferdinand Koch had called Nancy.

"I could hear him across the room," said George, "and I wasn't even on the phone with him!"

"He was pretty upset," agreed Nancy. "He said it was the first time he'd ever bought forgeries. You know, I'm sort of sorry we found out about his police record. He's really a bad kid turned good adult. *Very* good adult."

"I bet he doesn't even care that the missing street scene was returned now that he knows it's a forgery," George added.

Nancy shook her head, smiling. "No, he doesn't. Although *I* do. I like to have all the loose ends of a mystery tied up."

Koch had called Nancy to talk about Devereaux's arrest. But he had also had an interesting piece of news for her. A security guard had been caught *returning* the missing street scene earlier that morning. He had accidentally knocked it off the wall the night before it was reported stolen and had broken the frame. He'd panicked and had taken the painting home to try to repair it. He'd hoped to return it without being caught—but he hadn't succeeded. The missing cuff link was his, he admitted. He didn't know anything about the live bat, though.

"Imagine a bat loose in a museum!" Bess exclaimed.

"Poor thing," said George.

"Poor thing?" Bess said indignantly. "Poor thing, my foot. I'll never go into a museum again!"

"Mariel Devereaux is going to have her surgery," Brian spoke up quietly. "Dad and my grandfather are arranging for it right now. She didn't know anything about what her father was up to." He paused. "I can't believe my father and grandfather are actually working *together*. It's all because of the diary. I have you to thank for that, Nancy."

Nancy looked at Ned, and they exchanged a private smile. After a long discussion they had decided to give Danielle's diary to the Seatons. "Mr. Westlake and Mr. Seaton both loved Danielle," Nancy had told Ned. "They loved her so much they've been rushing around trying to raise money just to get her portrait back. All those meetings, Ned—they were attempts to raise ransom money."

"Except the time Mr. Seaton disappeared during the ball."

"Right. I guess that really was some kind of private business. But if they both loved Danielle so much," Nancy had said, "I guess they both should know the truth about her, and about the accident."

"I think so too," Ned had replied.

Mr. Seaton had been shocked, of course, when he found out about Danielle's illness, and even more shocked when Nancy told him her theory about the accident. But he had been slightly relieved, too. And he had called Mr. Westlake to give him the news and to try to reconcile things.

"I've got you to thank for something else, too," Brian said to Nancy.

"What's that?" Nancy put her sunglasses on so she could see Brian better.

"The portrait. Mariel Devereaux said she wanted *me* to have it. Warren Tyler doesn't want it, now that he knows it's not really my mother. But I don't remember my mom well, anyway, so it doesn't matter to me. It'll just be nice to have *Danielle's Dream*. Maybe someday my father will be able to look at pictures of my mother again. Then if he wants the painting, I'll give it to him."

"That's nice," commented Bess. "I like happy endings. And the ending to this case is pretty happy."

"For everyone except Max Devereaux," George pointed out.

"But even he's getting what he wanted . . . sort of," Ned said. "Mariel will have her surgery."

"And Dad and grandfather are getting to be

friends," added Brian. "Maybe Warren and Dad will become friends, too."

"And you got *Danielle's Dream*," said George.

"And Bess got a tan," added Nancy.

Everyone laughed.

"I hereby invite you all back next year," Brian said. "For Mardi Gras. Will you come?"

"*Will* we?" exclaimed Nancy. "We wouldn't miss it for the world!"

RECEIVED
NOV 1 9 1999
VNA OF BOSTON